Absent:
The English Teacher

Absent:
The English Teacher

John Eppel

WEAVER
—PRESS—

Published by
Weaver Press, Box A1922, Avondale, Harare. 2009

© John Eppel, 2009

Typeset by Weaver Press
Cover Design: banana republic
Printed by Pinetown Printers, Johannesburg

The publishers would like to express their gratitude to HIVOS
for the support they have given to
Weaver Press in the development of their
fiction programme.

ISBN: 978 1 77922 082 0

Born in South Africa in 1947, John Eppel was raised in Zimbabwe, where he still lives, making his home in Bulawayo near the Matobo Hills. He teaches English at Christian Brothers College. His first novel, *D.G.G. Berry's The Great North Road*, won the M-Net prize in South Africa and was listed in the *Weekly Mail & Guardian* as one of the best 20 South African books in English published between 1948 and 1994. His second novel, *Hatchings*, was short-listed for the M-Net prize and was chosen for the series in the *Times Literary Supplement* of the most significant books to have come out of Africa. His other novels include *The Giraffe Man*, *The Curse of the Ripe Tomato*, and *The Holy Innocents*. His book of poems, *Spoils of War*, won the Ingrid Jonker Prize. His other poetry books include *Sonata for Matabeleland, Selected Poems: 1965-1995*, and *Songs My Country Taught Me*. In addition he has written two books which combine poems and short stories: *The Caruso of Colleen Bawn*, and *White Man Crawling*. Awaiting publication is a book of poems entitled *Landlocked*, and a book of short stories entitled *White Man Walking*.

CONTENTS

John Eppel and the Place of Literature in the Postcolonial World

Kizito Z. Muchemwa

It is not often that one reads a Zimbabwean novel that provides such a wide range of pleasures to its readers. *Absent: The English Teacher* by John Eppel displays an exhilarating verbal agility (which lends the novel much of its humour); a powerful evocation of place and historical period; and the vivid creation of memorable characters. His plot's construction draws on a rich linguistic inventiveness, his denotations and connotations of words leading the narrator, the (former) English teacher, to new incidents, thoughts and feelings. A sense of the incongruous and grasp of historical detail are also connected as language, characters and events are connected in a web of their referential and allusive power. The narrator has the comic genius of Feste and Hamlet, and this allows him to see all kinds of possible connections in a world that has gone awry. Satire, arising out of a compulsive play on words as both a mental disposition and a mode of viewing a cock-eyed reality, allows the writer to use humour therapeutically as the narrator engages with actuality.

Eppel creates vivid landscapes that provide the setting for his novels: landscape that is invested in the weight of historical and cultural memory, a contested site for the location of identities in an endless cycle of migration and displacement. It also represents many aspects of ecology: its diversity, its miraculous capacity to sustain life, and its fragility. Nature, in the raw, reveals that landscapes are far from idyllic despite the tender evocation of the acacia savannah surrounding Bulawayo. What emerges from these descriptions is not only Eppel's intimate knowledge and love of the local flora and fauna but an abiding concern for the environment; he brings into his writing the expertise of the botanist, ornithologist, zoologist and game ranger. In *Absent: the English Teacher*, the suburban garden becomes a site of what George describes as 'ecological imperialism', as well as a symbol of change in the country's history. Ironically, when Mrs Nyamayakanuna invades George's suburban home she makes sure that all the indigenous fruit trees, previously planted by George, are destroyed leaving only exotic ones. The traditional 'English' garden is transformed into a maize patch. The agents of change are not flattered for their actions.

Eppel makes his flat characters the butt of his satire, though in some respects they also provide the novel's moral centre. His ingenious use of names provide condensed exposés of characteristics that we at once recognise and find ridiculous: Mrs d'Artagnan-Mararike; Minister of Child Welfare, Sweets and Biscuits, Comrade Pontius Gonzo; Mrs Beauticious Nyamayakanuna; the twins Helter and Skelter, and a school girl named City Lights. He plays with names to convey psychological and moral attributes. Possessions are assumed as accessories of personality, markers of ethical and aesthetic positions.

Collapsing the distinction between the historical and imagined allows for entertaining inventiveness in plot construction. Historical and invented occurrences are recast and amplified to create a fictional world in which the incredible happens. Change turns a white school teacher into a domestic servant for a black family; the black madam, in a parody of her white forebears, speaks to the white lackey in Kitchen Kaffir and forbids him to speak to her in English; cabinet ministers maintain a string of mistresses; and wilfully destructive programmes are foisted on the country by a reckless and ruthless elite. If there is a whiff of improbability, it must be remembered that the comic mode that dominates the novel thrives on its capacity to stretch credibility to the limit. Zimbabweans need no reminding, however, that the so-called real world has recently been shaped by what most people would understand as the incredible and unimaginable.

In *Absent: The English Teacher* the writer mocks the excesses: corruption, vulgarity, greed, and insensitivity of the new black elite. He unhesitatingly refers to those events which he sees as characteristic of both the tragedy and the comedy that is post-independence Zimbabwe – the ethnic cleansing in Matabeleland during the 1980s, political repression, absence of the rule of law after 2000, the general collapse of the economy and services, man-made famine, the pauperisation of workers and professionals, and the amazing greed of the *nouveau riche*.

George, the school teacher, come down in the world, and as such becomes a synecdoche of white Zimbabwean identity, a victim of a xenophobic invasion of urban properties and now the domestic servant of a mistress of the Minister of Child Welfare, Sweets and Biscuits. He tells his pupils, 'They say there's always an ironic gap between author and persona, but I'm not so sure, really… not so sure.' This can be read as an admission that the novel includes autobiographical features. Self-writing occurs in a post-2000 Zimbabwe that has become increasingly politicised, impoverished, vulgarised, and brutalised. Neither the fictional narrator nor the writer can escape this historical context, and this is the subject of this novel. Literature of commitment calls for the self-implication of writers in the ethical demands of their times. Eppel illustrates this in his exploration of the instability of genres.

Literary genres rarely have clear boundaries but ones that collapse, blur and merge. The novel that is ostensibly satirical in conception and method insists on exceeding satire. Eppel shows that satire, tragedy, and comedy are premised on instability and paradox. This allows the writer to treat life as an oxymoron and to view it in its complexity. Consequently, this leads him to contain the horrors of life, to put up with random violence and various forms of dispossession and displacement in both real life and within a fictional experience in the novel. *Absent: The English Teacher* is a multi-layered novel: autobiography, historical fiction, satire, inverted pastoral, and a parody of an adventure story constantly crossing the formal and stylistic boundaries separating prose fiction from drama. There are so many literary motifs and intertextual references that this text is an ideal, even exemplary, 'literary' novel. It would, however, be a mistake to think that it has little significance beyond its aesthetic 'games'. At every turn, the novel demands that the aesthetic and ethical aspects of literary creativity be integrated. It is as much about literature of ethical commitment and responsibility as it is a literary novel in which the writer is engaged in formal and linguistic games. As with autobiography there are many areas where it becomes difficult to separate the fictive from the historical and the separation is perhaps not necessary for it would detract from the novel's effectiveness. Eppel, like Marechera, brings to the Zimbabwean novel vast erudition and a sure sense of style.

The novel begins as a farewell to the class of uninspired learners, and combines comic and sad moments, though it returns to the concept of 'teacher' in reconstructed circumstances. A textual reference, one not signalled in this text but filled with intertextual clues and references, is Evelyn Waugh's *Decline and Fall*,[1] a satirical attack on the vacuity, venality, snobbery, and lack of feeling found in the public school system in England of that time. Much of the humour in Waugh's novel relates to the school as a site for the articulation of bourgeois ennui, indolence, greed and cruelty. The motif of decline and fall is, I believe, modelled on Waugh's novel. Eppel, similarly, mocks the caricature of school he portrays in the novel.

Although, most of the references are to canonical English literature texts, the writer crosses cultural boundaries to include the fiction of Ngugi wa Thiongo, firmly placing his novels within the tradition of good literature in English and the universality of good literature *per se*. In this regard the cultural baggage that George carries is consistent with his concern with identity as it relates to this important aspect of cultural production. George is fired from Boys and Girls Come Out to Play Secondary School for behaviour deemed to be inconsistent with the demands of his profession. This departure compels him to begin a truly post-colonial reconstruction of identity that, ironically, is conceived in the discourse of Aristotelian aesthetics and Elizabethan drama. George progressively divests himself, Lear fashion, of cultural trappings that provide a false identity and in the Zimbabwean bush he confronts himself and his past. He can only become another when he returns to his origins where he symbolically burns the envelope containing his identity as a teacher and a putative Englishman.

The close reading of literary texts becomes an empowering tool that can be turned to scrutinise discourses of domination. The rigorous linguistic scrutiny of texts that the English teacher demonstrates is not very different from the creativity it mediates. The teacher describes Hamlet as 'a great punster, a great imitator, a lover of paradoxes', a cap that would fit Eppel very well. A word, a telling detail of the world around the main character, allows for flights of fancy that call for every imaginable figure of speech in a novel that uses its literariness to engage with life in contemporary Zimbabwe, a country characterised by absence of beauty, hatred, lack of moderation, insanity, and a surprising capacity for the tragically absurd. Citizens are subjected to arbitrary arrest by an arrogant and poorly educated police. The prisons into which they are thrown are overcrowded and unsanitary. In a way the novel is an anti-epic that provides a cockroach vision of society, exposing that which is hidden by propaganda, and statutory and administrative instruments.

The texts that dominate the novel are *Hamlet* and *King Lear*. References and allusions to such historical drama colour setting, characterisation, and themes. These plays are among other things about politics, power, change, and crises of identity and demonstrate that, contrary to certain misconceptions, literature is not divorced from life. Its aesthetic and formal aspects are central to its creation of meaning and its connection with reality. At this level, *Absent: The English Teacher* reflects an ethical-political demand to 'doing justice to and being responsible to and for the other'[2]. George responds to this demand by rejecting the limitations of a canon that excludes the other. The Lear-like experience allows him to recognise the need for a selfless love that brings justice into a generally unjust world full of gratuitous violence, one in which the ordinary citizen is turned into a howling Tom of the heath. This is the catharsis that occurs in the world. The collapse of the world of privilege prepares the ground for self-knowledge and the exercise of agape. The recognition of the other begins when George is arrested, after the comic debacle of switched portraits, and comes face to face with prisoners of a rogue regime. A second arrest ensures that this recognition of the other is sustained. This prepares the reader for the entry of the abandoned child. Her rescue combines several motifs that deal with the other. Polly Petal is Perdita, the lost daughter that George never had, Cordelia who gets reconciled to George when everything has been lost, a figure of the black other, and an object of love. This demand goes beyond the limitations of what, in retrospect, is Robert Mugabe's defective, expedient, and Machiavellian policy of reconciliation, crafted by reason and not the heart.

References to Shakespeare's plays reinforce Eppel's view of the limitations of conventional genres and forms and their inability to contain lived experience. They are also meant to establish the play between actual and imagined worlds. Genres and forms are prisons from which writers, like prisoners of state tyranny, try to escape. The prison motif in Hamlet and the movement from the court to the heath in *King Lear* parallel the displacement from a centre of privilege to the bushveld.

John Eppel's comic style is very much in tune with Augustan satire as the 'art of sinking'; it is partisan and employs every tool in satire's arsenal to demolish the position of political and cultural opponents. The butts of his previous satire have mainly focused on various versions of white Rhodesian identity. After metaphorically killing off this subject in *The Holy Innocents* and *The Curse of the Ripe Tomato*,³ he has surprisingly come to resurrect it in this his latest offering, where he also turns his humour on the new black political elite. Parody is a technique that requires a sure grasp of genre, form, and style, but it allows him to laugh at some of the inbuilt assumptions and shortcomings of specific literary traditions. Parody provides a comic lens through which the writer interprets life. In Eppel's use of this form, art imitates art, life imitates art, and art imitates life, providing some hilarious incongruities as he explores the tragic-comic aspects of old and new identities in post-colonial Zimbabwe.

Of special interest are the constructions of white identity in Zimbabwe and their displacement at sites of power and privilege by the black nouveau riche. The writer inserts his own biography into the fiction and turns himself into a synecdoche, a scapegoat for sins of commission and omission in a dramatic role reversal and enactment of *King Lear, Hamlet,* and *Macbeth.* The ploy broadens the scope and quality of the satire and entails a spirit of generosity by this self-implication in Rhodesian white identity. Eppel is able to laugh not only at other people but also at himself, making the comedy richly Falstaffian. He is also gratuitously made to carry the sins of his race in a Zimbabwe currently obsessed by racial intolerance.

The epic journey in reverse to Empandeni Mission and Fort Mangwe is one of re-discovery and restitution. It also allows the writer to articulate his identity as a white Ndebele with a deep and intimate knowledge of what colonialists and those who have displaced them have constructed as Matabeleland. Apart from running through the litany of ethnic wrongs, this construction is not problematised and it would not be proper here to expect more than what he offers.

My lasting impressions of *Absent: The English Teacher*, despite the topicality of the political and social issues it raises, are that it is about the following – justifying English literary studies in the academy, the role of literature in mediating reality, literature as an analgesic in an age of violence and insecurity, the consolations of autobiography in an economically and culturally degraded environment, and the limits and possibilities of humour. A certain degree of erudition is a precondition for fully appreciating Eppel's mixed grill of comedy and tragedy, heroism and bathos, seriousness and levity. Playfulness, a central aspect of humour, may find the writer consistently denying any gravity to many of the issues that are raised in the text. No subject is taboo.

The book should be read mainly as an autobiographical take on the joys and frustrations of teaching English, the relevance of English literature at tertiary level and in post-colonial society, and a sober reflection on the achievements of a lifetime. It is also a more than useful Glossary of Literary Terms and English Usage. In addition, there is a very persuasive reading of the historical background that has shaped Elizabethan drama, especially the role of Francis Walsingham's 'complex system of espionage' as 'secret theatre'. It is an analysis that will help readers to understand the fear, insecurity, and staged events in Zimbabwe that are associated with the dominance of the secret service, through propaganda and in the war against opposition and civic figures. This openly ethical approach to literature occurs when the writer takes off the chev'ril gloves, a new development that brings him closer to African writers of commitment. The text veers between Dambudzo Marechera in its concern with technique and Ngugi wa Thiongo in its fierce engagement with the political. It is clear that in the end Eppel chooses the route of open commitment. *Absent: the English Teacher* has more similarities with *Wizard of the Crow*,[4] in which wa Thiongo is simultaneously a great fabulator and fierce critic of the flaws and excesses of the post-colonial state in Africa, than with his earlier novel, *A Grain of Wheat*.[5]

References

1. Evelyn Waugh. *Decline and Fall*. London: Heinemann Educational Books, 1966 | 1928|.

2 Michael Eskin. Introduction: 'The Double "Turn" to Ethics and Literature?' *Poetics Today*, 25:4 557-572.

3 John Eppel. *The Holy Innocents*. Bulawayo, 'amaBooks, 2002; *The Curse of the Ripe Tomato*, 'amaBooks, 2001.

4 Ngugi wa Thiongo. *Wizard of the Crow*. London: Vintage, 2007 [2006].

5 Ngugi wa Thiongo. *A Grain of Wheat*. Oxford: Heinemann Educational Books, 1983.

FOR CONNY,
WHO INTRODUCED ME TO
WHITE-BROWED
SPARROW-WEAVERS.

1

PALE MOON RISING

When George J. George mistook his white Ford Escort for the moon, he knew that his time was up. He would turn his face to the evening star and, guided by the nests of white-browed sparrow-weavers, keep walking. Would he walk alone?

"Mr George!" hissed the headmaster turning from the podium in mid-speech to face the errant school-teacher, who still had the straw in his mouth – "you will see me without fail first thing tomorrow morning! In my office, Mr George!" Then he turned back to the auditorium and proceeded with his speech as if nothing untoward had happened. George pushed the straw down the neck of the bottle and surreptitiously screwed on the blue cap. He kept his beetroot-coloured face busy scanning his knee-caps and those of the teachers sitting on his immediate left and right. He was for it!

So, Mrs Maphosa is wearing a tartan skirt! Wonder what clan it represents? George was only half listening to the headmaster droning on about sporting achievements… er… inflation… er… Friday detention… er… how honoured the school would be to host the Deputy Secretary of Education and Urban (sic) Beauty Pageants… er… the immeasurable contribution to the running of the school by the prefects (most of them sons and daughters of board members)… er… the support he constantly received, in these times of trial and tribulation from his dogs, Bella and Fella (Grey Street terriers who were notorious for stealing sandwiches from the pupils' school bags), and… er… last but not least… er… his secretary, Miss Poops who… er… short of darning his socks… er… was like a mother to him… er… (tremendous applause from His Worship the Mayor, distinguished guests, parents, and those pupils who did not have access to play stations and who were, consequently, still capable of sentimentality).

Half preparing a lesson for his A-Level English class, Mrs Maphosa's skirt reminded him of Andrew Marvell's scurrilous depiction of the Scots in his 'Horatian Ode':

> *The pict no shelter now shall find*
> *Within his parti-coloured mind;*
> *But from this valour sad*
> *Shrink underneath the plaid:*
> *Happy if in the tufted brake*
> *The English hunter him mistake;*
> *Nor lay his hounds in near*
> *The Caledonian deer.*

His pupils couldn't understand why he found these lines so funny, so he had to explain (did you, though, George, did you really have to?) that 'shrink beneath the plaid' was an allusion to the penis under the kilt, and that 'mistake' – if you knew your Shakespeare – suggested adultery or, in this case, sodomy. How does Gower put it in *Henry* 5: 'Gentlemen, both, you will mistake each other.' And Jamy replies, 'A! That's a foul fault.' Suddenly the English soldier becomes the hunter while the Scottish soldier becomes the deer (dear). The hunt, boys and girls, is an allegory of sexual conquest.

But it was the moon, not a characteristic Marvell image (now we're in Coleridge territory), that haunted George, drunk as he was, after Speech Night. The ceremony had been held at the amphitheatre in the Centenary Park, and when George, shunned by colleagues and parents alike, but attracting some appreciative stares from the more rowdy element of school pupil, stumbled groggily out in search of his car – now where the heck did I park it? – he mistook a pale moon on the horizon for a white 1978 Ford Escort 1.3L .

George could not understand why his car seemed to recede as he approached it, keys in hand. As an English teacher he was familiar with paradoxes, *concordia discors* and all that. He could go on for hours about the necessity of opposites; that it was the dust that proved the sweetness of a shower; that you needed light to cast a shadow; that if it was the best of times, it was also the worst of times… paradoxes didn't scratch your face, skin your shin, stub your toe – useless bloody items… cardboard junk… transported on junks… juncque… junco… jonk…djong went his Chinese-made shoes as they negotiated anthills, plastic litter, rusty tins, dog and human turds, grass clumps, roots, chongololas and all the other things you'd expect your footwear to encounter in Bulawayo's Centenary Park, which straddles the road out to Johannesburg… where the rikki tikki tikki tram runs from Fordsburg, and the mine hooter tells you the time. He couldn't get that tune out of his head.

He stopped to take a swig from his straw-infiltrated bottle of Skipper cane (beer and wine had become too expensive for teachers, security guards and domestic workers) and suddenly realised that he had left the park and was heading vaguely in the direction of Gwanda. Wasn't that the Museum of Natural History on his left? He was lurching along Leopold Takawira Avenue, which he still called, in the dank recesses of his colonial mind, Selborne Avenue. Surely he hadn't parked the Ford so far away from the amphitheatre? Cripes, it's not my car, it's the moon. I've had it, finished, though I kept not the faith, though I fought not the good fight. It is time. Thus George, suddenly maudlin, half a bottle of cane spirit turning his tummy into a pinball machine.

He turned his back on the moon, though not his mind. Christabel watching Geraldine undress is Coleridge looking at the moon (snorts of incredulity from his pupils… why can't you just give us notes to learn, you old fart); the moon is a symbol of his creative imagination; it is female, moon, month, menses, the tenth muse:

> Beneath the lamp the lady bowed,
> And slowly rolled her eyes around;
> Then drawing in her breath aloud,
> Like one that shuddered, she unbound
> The cincture from beneath her breast:
> Her silken robe, and inner vest,
> Dropt to her feet, and full in view,
> Behold! her bosom and half her side –
> A sight to dream of, not to tell!
> O shield her! shield sweet Christabel.

The Heuglin's robin was tuning up for the dawn chorus by the time George found his car, parked a few metres from the Speech Night venue.

With no one around to give him a push, he collected his hammer from the boot and used it to give the starter motor a whack. He drove home tormented by that ear worm: where the rikki tikki tikki tram runs from Fordsburg...

2

A GLINT OF COPPER

That was some time before the event which began his rapid decline: the mischievous switching of portraits; and the event that accelerated his rapid decline: the accident in Robert Mugabe Way. George taught English at Boys and Girls Come Out to Play Secondary School, a private establishment situated in the not so leafy suburbs of Bulawayo. This school was to be visited by the Deputy Secretary for Education and Rural Beauty Pageants, and he was to be accompanied by an entourage of sixty government officials. Well, King Lear demanded a hundred; so what's the complaint? I mean! And don't forget Lear was retired, crawling his way toward death, not burdened with responsibilities like the Deputy Secretary whose oldest son, Fuchsware, had recently written off his parliamentary tractor, a Massey Ferguson if you please, just weeks before the mother of all agricultural seasons was about to begin! So if an Englishman can do it, why can't I? Besides, these private schools were renowned for the slap-up lunches they provided on politically sensitive occasions.

George had been entrusted with the job of making sure that the President's portrait would be hanging in any of the rooms that the Deputy Secretary cared to visit. Unfortunately there was only one portrait of the President. It used to hang in the school hall but was now nowhere to be found. George made the mistake of consulting the class for which he was Form teacher: 3 Remove, the bottom stream. The naughtiest boys and girls of the entire school were in this class, none naughtier than Ivan 'the terrible' McKaufmann. George should have smelt a rat when Ivan offered to help him find the missing portrait, but George was desperate, and exhausted.

The morning had begun with his Sixth Form class – a lesson on Emily Brontë's method of using dogs to further the plot of *Wuthering Heights*. The only way he could get these yahoos the slightest bit interested in their

Advanced Level set work was to portray Heathcliff as a werewolf and Cathy as a nymphomaniac. *Othello* was worse: he had to teach it as a comedy. As for Andrew Marvell: buggery, bestiality, paederasty – even a bit of normal sex. God knows what the Cambridge examiners made of his pupils' scripts. With glowing cheeks, he re-lived the lesson.

[Typical classroom hubbub over which George speaks. Distinct sound of Brenda Fassie singing 'Vulindela']

GEORGE: Cut that music! *[music stops]* Moyo, will you please stop tapping your pen on your tooth and answer my question?

MOYO: Sorry Sir. What was the question?

GEORGE: *[sighing with irritation]* How does the author use dogs to get Lockwood into the bed with panelled sides so that the crucial dream can take place?

MOYO: What dream, Sir?

GEORGE: Moyo, we've read it half a dozen times! You know, where Cathy symbolically loses her virginity. Quote: 'I pulled its wrist on to the broken pane, and rubbed it to and fro till the blood ran down and soaked the bedclothes…'

[A bunch of boys at the back begin to chant] Let her in, let her in, let her in…

GEORGE: Quiet! And it's 'me', not 'her'! Can anybody else answer my question?

MUKADAM: What question's that, Sir?

GEORGE: What do you mean 'what question's that'? Why aren't you paying attention?

CHORUS OF VOICES: It's Eid, Sir; he's fasting.

GEORGE: Well then, what about you, Sabina? How does Emily Brontë use dogs to get Lockwood into Cathy's old room?

SABINA: That bulldog bites her ankle, Sir…

GEORGE: No, no, no, Sabina. That's what gets Cathy in to Thrushcross Grange, where she meets her future hus-

JONES: Sir, does Edgar know that Cathy has lost her virginity when he asks her to marry him?

SIBANDA: Don't be stupid, man! Girls don't tell those things…

PARSHOTAM: They use chicken blood, don't they, Sir?

LERTITIA: Rubbish! You boys don't know what you talking about!

GEORGE: I…

VAN RENSBURG: Sir, was Heathcliff normal or was he a werewolf when he made love to Cathy?

SIBANDA: Don't be stupid, man. He did it at night so he must of been a werewolf.

GEORGE: I… boys, girls, can we get back to the question?

NEW PUPIL: *|amid chorus of voices:|* Sir! Sir! Sir!

GEORGE: Yes, er…

NEW PUPIL: He tied her Fanny with a hanky and then hung it in a tree.

GEORGE: What? Oh you mean Isabella's dog, who was called…er…Fanny? No, that's much later on in the novel; it signals the entering of Heathcliff into Isabella's bedroom; the night he elopes with her.

JONES: Do you think he banged her straight away, Sir?

|banging of desks in sympathy with this profound question. One boy cries out:| Let me in! *|much ribald laughter|*

GEORGE: *|panicking|* Quiet, quiet, QUIET! Will somebody answer my question?   Yes, er…

|pandemonium settles back into hubbub|

NEW PUPIL: I can't answer your question but I can think of another place in the novel where dogs further the plot.

|class becomes almost silent with expectation|

GEORGE: Go on then, er…

NEW PUPIL: *|last three words emphasised|* It's a dog fight that first brings Cathy's daughter and Hareton together. And that's when Hareton gives her one.

|Expectation satisfied. Rapidly silence ascends into murmur, noise, roar,

pandemonium. This gives George time to locate the place in the text, and when the class finally allows him, he speaks|

GEORGE: Yes, well done, er… here it is, page 231: |*reads*|'Hareton, recovering from his disgust at being taken for a servant, seemed moved by her distress; and, having fetched the pony round to the door, he took, to propitiate her, a fine crooked-legged terrier whelp from the kennel; and putting it into her hand …'

JONES: |*interrupting*| Sir, Sir, is the terrier a symbol of his willy?

GEORGE: How many times have I told you, Jones, that while there is no right and wrong in literary analysis, there is a good deal of intelligence. You have to be convincing.

JONES: Well, but is it?

GEORGE: Is it what?

JONES: A symbol.

GEORGE: More a motif than a symbol, I should think. Sometimes it's implied. If you turn to page 302 you'll see what I mean. |*The three pupils who have brought their texts to class turn to page 302. George reads*| 'It's odd what a savage feeling I have to anything that seems afraid of me'. Here Heathcliff clearly compares himself to a dog.

SIBANDA: Well, he's a werewolf, which is a kind of a dog!

GEORGE: There's no absolute proof …

The bell signalling the end of the period came to George's rescue, and he slumped onto his desk while the pupils fought their way noisily out of the classroom. He had a minute or two, before the next class, to empty his mind of literary dogs and refill it with images of the unattainable: his enchantress… he wished her name were Laura or Beatrice, or even Lamia; Wilhelmine did not conform to the convention, to the vision of vanilla-scented candles illuminating a skin of purest alabaster.

His next class was beginning to arrive. |*slightly higher pitched voices*| The noise was deafening. George checked his timetable.

GEORGE: |*muted voice*| Form Three. What are we doing? 'Kubla Khan'. Oh no! More sex! Damn that fountain with its dancing rocks, those sinuous rills … |*normal voice*| Morning class! |*loud voice*| I said good morning, class!

CHORUS OF VOICES: Morning Sir. What are we doing today?

GEORGE: Coleridge.

MUGABE: But Sir, he's a pervert!

GEORGE: He's not a pervert, Mugabe, he's a visionary, a seer; like Orpheus, he sings the world into being…

McKAUFMANN: What about that pleasure dome, then? You said it's a fanny.

GEORGE: I didn't use the word 'fanny', McKaufmann, I…

McKAUFMANN: Yes you did, Sir, and I told my father, and he says he wants to have a word with you.

GEORGE: Well, he knows where to find me. Now, class, listen:

> In Xanadu did Kubla Khan a stately pleasure-dome decree,
> Where Alph the…

MAGATE: Sir, Sir!

GEORGE [irritated]: Yes, Magate?

MAGATE: I've got an uncle called Alf. He drives a Pajero.

GEORGE: Indeed! Now please stop interrupting and listen!

> Where Alph, the sacred river, ran
> Through caverns measureless to man…

Who can find an example of hyperbole, exaggeration for effect, in those lines?

NAIK: Yes, Sir.

GEORGE: Go on, Naik.

NAIK: It's 'cavern', Sir.

GEORGE: Why?

NAIK: 'Cause a cavern is huge compared to a fanny.

[ribald laughter]

NOTHANDO: Sir, Sir!

GEORGE: Yes, Nothando?

NOTHANDO: Can we watch a video?

9

GEORGE: You can but you may not!

McKAUFMANN: Ah Sir, why not?

GEORGE: Because we have work to do; and put your sandwiches away; it isn't time for break.

VOICES: But Sir! Sir!

GEORGE: /yells/QUIET! By the way, does anybody know what happened to the President's portrait that used to hang in the hall?

That's how the lesson began; that's how it went on, and that's how it ended. During the break which followed this lesson, George had to drink four cups of tea to steady his nerves, which were being frayed not only by the real world but by the vividness of his ineffable yearning. That's a good phrase. He might use it in a sequence of sonnets he was busy composing for the elusive Wilhelmine. George first met Wilhelmine at a gathering of NGOs and their 'partners'. It was held around the swimming pool of Wilhelmine's house, a bring-and-braai party. You brought chunks of bloody red meat, which you scorched on the open fire, and bottles of beer and red wine, which you drank, frequently, straight from the bottle. Although Wilhelmine was then 'seeing' a fellow NGO (she did borehole pumps, he did small grains) she showed a genuine interest in George: part of a sub-culture now no longer so vilified because almost extinct, known as Rhodies. And George was not typical of the breed, being… er… a poet.

That day she spent a lot more time with him than she did with Small Grains. They talked about consciousness and the necessity of opposites: *Leben und Tod*; and as the shadows lengthened across the lawn they occasionally held each other's gaze, occasionally touched: a wrist, or an elbow, or a knee-cap. Once, briefly, their spectacles became entangled. She smelt pure, somehow: of aloe vera. When it grew dark, Wilhelmine brought out a large white candle, lit it and placed it between them. Then the moon began to rise, and George was smitten. It had been love almost at first sight. Dangerously he excluded from his vision the reality of Small Grains, a child of seven fathered by Oxfam Canada, and a dog that would play no small role in the unfolding plot. For example, it bit him twice, which resulted in Wilhelmine attending to him in a manner which he misinterpreted; it, not he, was the reason for some romantic walks in the bush on the outskirts of town; it, not he, was the reason for George's providing the Oxfam Canada child's kitten with a safe house. The subsequent visits to his home by the enchanting Teuton and her child were for the kitten's sake, not his.

All that was still to come. Now, in the magical glow of the scented white candle, the orange moon gazing at its reflection in the swimming pool, the murmur of NGOs from all over the world, and their mostly Shona or Ndebele 'partners', George confessed his undying love to Wilhelmine. She gave his Achilles tendon a playful squeeze and then warned him tenderly that she could not give him what he wanted; she was not some moon goddess; she was an inhabitant of the murky waters of reality, a slimy crawling thing, a red frog! Perversely, her self-denial made George even more convinced that Wilhelmine was the moon personified, and his creative imagination began to process sonnets. When the party finally came to an end, it was Small Grains, not George, who stayed for the night.

Over the next few weeks they met intermittently, when Small Grains was out in the rural areas encouraging the peasants to plant small grains instead of maize. The reality of these meetings was a few beers, a snack or two, a little bit of hand-holding, and perhaps a fumbled kiss. But the vision, for George, was paradisal. Even the child and the dog were transformed into winged creatures, while the rather scrubby garden and the algae-infested swimming pool became the Elysian Fields. It was during the school holidays that Wilhelmine was to attend an NGO retreat in Botswana. What alarmed George was that Small Grains was to accompany her. His jealousy began to rival Othello's, though he stopped short of epileptic fits. Later he was to learn that Small Grains was just that in Wilhelmine's repertoire of lovers.

The Deputy Minister and his entourage of plump, beautifully attired (on credit) officials were on their way to the metalwork classroom, outside which George anxiously waited, hammer and steel nail in hand, when McKaufmann arrived with the portrait inside a large Mr Price shopping bag. There was no time to lose. George drove in the nail, just to the left of the blackboard; his pupil hung the portrait, and then promptly disappeared. George didn't even have a chance to thank him.

For contributing to his ruin. It was Mrs d'Artagnan-Mararike (accounts at Edgars, Truworths, Meikles, Power Sales – by arrangement – and The Forgotten Woman) who first noticed the coppery portrait of Ian Smith. She screamed and dropped the drumstick she had been nibbling. Then, one by one, her colleagues noticed the abomination, and two of them managed to drag it down before the Deputy Secretary, who had been talking on his cellphone, noticed. Lying smashed on the floor, his bland profile winking at the many pairs of costly shoes that gathered around, as if trying to determine which were crocodile hide, which elephant, which python, which ostrich, which – but those belong to Mr George – reinforced cardboard. Lying there, Ian Smith looked more pathetic than threatening. Consequently, the Deputy Secretary reacted with amusement rather than anger. Fawning officialdom took his cue, and the metalwork room rang with the laughter of ridicule. George thought he was off the hook but he had a nasty surprise in store.

3

A WEEKEND IN ELSINORE

Scene 1: *George J. George's house, suburban Bulawayo, late Friday afternoon. George is lying on his back on the lounge carpet, a quart of Castle lager within reach, listening enraptured to his record player. The music is Richard Strauss's 'Vier Letzte Lieder', sung by Elisabeth Schwartzkopf. George's pets are with him. The cat is on his tummy, the dog at his feet, and the hen, busily preening, at his head.*

Just as the final song, 'Im Abendrot', begins, a hooter sounds at the gate. It is long and insistent. The dog growls |YOU MIGHT HAVE TO USE A RECORDING FOR THIS|, *George sighs and sits up, disturbing the cat. The hen continues to preen itself.*

GEORGE: Who comes round on a Friday afternoon?

The hooting continues. George gets up reluctantly and goes to stop the music. He takes a long swallow of beer from the brown bottle before slamming it down.

Exits lounge with all three pets following: |IF POSSIBLE| *first the dog, then the cat, then the hen.*

CURTAIN

Scene 2: *The garden of George's home. George and pets looking expectant. Offstage: sound of gate latch, gate creaks open, diesel engine, neutral, then first gear, tyres on gravel, ENTER Land Rover, stops midstage, neutral gear, front passenger window slides down. There are three police officers in the vehicle, two men and a woman (the driver).*

OFFICER: Mr George?

GEORGE: Yes?

OFFICER: Mr George George?

GEORGE: Yes.

OFFICER: Mr George J. George of 43 Leander Avenue, Hillside, Bulawayo?

GEORGE: Yes. What is this? Are you the police? Are you-

OFFICER: You are wanted down at the charge office for questioning.

GEORGE: About what? Are you arresting me?

[Back door of Land Rover opens.]

OFFICER: Get in, Mr George.

GEORGE: On what charges? Do you have a warrant?

OFFICER: Would you like my friends here to help you get in, Mr George?

GEORGE: I need to make a phone call.

OFFICER: No you don't. Get in and let us go.

George looks vaguely about him and then climbs meekly into the vacant back seat of the vehicle, which revs, changes gear, and drives off. George's dog begins to howl. [YOU MIGHT HAVE TO USE A RECORDING FOR THIS.]

CURTAIN

Scene 3: *Virtual darkness. Overcrowded prison cell, downtown. Late Friday evening. Muted sounds especially coughing, clearing phlegm, sighing, shuffling, occasional groaning. Trapped flies buzzing. Distant traffic including ambulance and police sirens. Inmates packed like sardines.*

FIRST PRISONER (OLD MAN): We are not used to seeing a white man in this hotel. Why are you here?

GEORGE: I don't know, really. I think it's something to do with an incident that took place at my school on Wednesday.

SECOND PRISONER (YOUNGER MAN): You are a teacher?

GEORGE: I guess so. They say I have insulted the President, and that I have been causing alarm and despondency in the minds of the people…*[A terrible scream. Cell goes silent for a few seconds.]*

My God! What's that?

SECOND PRISONER: That must be MDC. They are torturing these opposition youths. You too must be voting for MDC.

GEORGE: Why do you say that?

SECOND PRISONER: You are white. All whites are voting for MDC.

GEORGE: I don't belong to any party. Cripes, how do you sleep in this place when there isn't even standing room?

FIRST PRISONER: We are taking it in turns to lie down.

GEORGE: Don't we even get blankets?

SECOND PRISONER: We get nothing.

GEORGE: Cripes, it stinks in here!

SECOND PRISONER: The toilet is blocked. Shit everywhere.

FIRST PRISONER: One toilet for thirty men and all of us are having diarrhoea.

GEORGE: Do we get fed? Not that I've got much of an appetite.

SECOND PRISONER: Once a day they bring a big dish of mealie-meal porridge.

[Sound of keys. Cell door creaks open.]

VOICE OF AUTHORITY: Mr George J. George!

SECOND PRISONER: It is your turn.

FIRST PRISONER: Do not worry. They are not beating whites.

GEORGE: What do you mean?

FIRST PRISONER: You will see. Better go now.

CURTAIN

Scene 4: *Interrogation room. Predictably unfurnished, with blood and other bodily discharges on the walls. George sits at one end of a battered table. Two interrogators in plain clothes and dark glasses face him from the other end. Palpable silence for several seconds. One of the interrogators is impatiently tapping a ball-point pen. A chair scrapes.*

FIRST INTERROGATOR: I repeat, are you a racist?

GEORGE: Yes. I hate the human race.

FIRST INTERROGATOR: So you hate black people?

GEORGE: Insofar as they are members of the human race, yes.

FIRST INTERROGATOR: Yes, what?

GEORGE: I… er… hate them.

FIRST INTERROGATOR: Who is 'them', Mr George?

GEORGE: Look, I wasn't being serious. I don't really hate the human race.

FIRST INTERROGATOR: I am waiting for an answer, Mr George.

GEORGE: I tell you, it was a joke, I have… er… I teach…

SECOND INTERROGATOR: Mr George, why did you hang a portrait of Ian Smith in your classroom?

GEORGE: It wasn't my classroom; it was metalwork, and…

SECOND INTERROGATOR: I repeat, why did you hang a portrait of that imperialist swine, Ian Smith, in your classroom?

GEORGE: It was a mistake. McKaufmann…

SECOND INTERROGATOR: Are you calling me a kaffirman?

GEORGE: No, no… McKaufmann. Ivan. He …

FIRST INTERROGATOR: You called my colleague a kaffirman. I heard you!

GEORGE: No, I… please…

FIRST INTERROGATOR: Enough, Mr George. I think it proves my point that you are a racist.

GEORGE: But …

FIRST INTERROGATOR: First, you insult our sovereign state by what is tantamount to an act of treason: replacing Our Excellency's portrait with one of that monster who murdered and raped millions of black people – men, women, and children. Second, you have the brazen effrontery to call my colleague a kaffirman. Third… er…you are causing alarm and despondency among the aboriginal peoples of Zimbabwe.

GEORGE: With respect, the Bushmen are long gone…

SECOND INTERROGATOR: Bushmen! Bushmen, Mr George! Is there no limit to your racial hatred?

GEORGE: Sorry… San. *[Sound of terrible screaming from another room, then silence for five seconds. George is visibly shaken.]*

SECOND INTERROGATOR: San! San! What is San?

GEORGE: Khoi San?

FIRST INTERROGATOR: It troubles me, George, that there is no sign of remorse in you. If it weren't for the Chief Inspector, who needs you to have a clear mind when he interviews you later, you would feel the back of my hand.

SECOND INTERROGATOR: And mine. Before we send you back to your cell, I want you to tell us where you got hold of that copper portrait of Ian Douglas Smith. Do you realise that it is now a collector's item and worth a lot of money?

GEORGE: I honestly don't know. McK… Ivan… gave it to me in a Mr Price shopping bag.

SECOND INTERROGATOR: Do you know how we can get hold of this Ivan?

GEORGE: Yes, he's at my school: Boys and Girls Come Out to Play. I can easily put you in contact with him.

SECOND INTERROGATOR: Good. You see, I am a collector of Rhodesiana. The stuff fetches a fortune in other countries. Last week I sold a 'Rhodesia is Super' T-shirt for five pounds sterling.

GEORGE: [now visibly relieved] I'll see what I can do.

FIRST INTERROGATOR: That's enough. Call the guards.

SECOND INTERROGATOR: *Mugadhijeri!*

CURTAIN

Scene 5: *Some time has passed. Inmates either lie packed together on their sides or stand in rows [George's position], waiting for their turn to sleep. Whistle.*

VOICE : *Chinja! Pindura!*

Shuffling sounds, groans, as people get to their feet or proceed to lie down.

GEORGE: What's he say?

FIRST PRISONER: He says it is time for changing over. Now we can be lying down for half hour.

SECOND PRISONER: No, not on your back; on your side.

GEORGE: Like sardines. Cripes, this place stinks. I feel like vomiting.

SECOND PRISONER: If you vomit they will make you eating it off the floor. Think about nice things.

GEORGE: Like what?

SECOND PRISONER: Like Coca-Cola.

GEORGE: How long have you been here?

SECOND PRISONER: I am forgetting. Very long time. Since last year.

GEORGE: Why are you here?

SECOND PRISONER: I was buying some forex from vapostori.

GEORGE: And you...er...?

FIRST PRISONER: They use POSA. They say we are having political rally. But we were just drinking some scuds outside the bottle store there by Hillside.

[Terrible scream from distant cell. Grunts, groans, and sighs of discomfort from inmates trying to make themselves comfortable on their sides on the filthy stone floor. Intermittent.]

GEORGE: And how long have you been here?

FIRST PRISONER: Sometimes... it is nearly one year now. Yes. Too long.

[Cell door opens]

VOICE: *Murungu!*

SECOND PRISONER: That is you.

GEORGE: Me again?

VOICE: *Murungu!*

[George battles to get up off the floor. Mutterings of apology.]

VOICE: Do not keep the Chief Inspector waiting.

GEORGE: Coming. Excuse me. Excuse me. Sorry...

CURTAIN

Scene 6 *Another interrogation Room. Brenda Fassie singing 'Vulindela'. Chief Inspector perusing a copy of* Hamlet *– cover visible to audience. Knock on door.*

CHIEF INSPECTOR: Come! *[Door opens, guard escorts George into room, guard exits]* Ah, Mr George... come in, come in. Take a chair.

18

[George mumbles something and sits down] How do you like your ac-commodation?

GEORGE: It's overcrowded and it stinks unbearably.

CHIEF INSPECTOR: Do you feel 'cabin'd, cribb'd, and confin'd'?

GEORGE: 'Bound in to saucy doubts and fears.'

CHIEF INSPECTOR: I knew I had found the right man. *[Puts down his copy of* Hamlet, *turns off the music.]* When I heard that you were coming in for questioning I told my people to be easy on you. You see I have this assignment to do for the Open University, and I have to sub-mit it by Monday. I need your help.

GEORGE: What's it on?

CHIEF INSPECTOR: *Hamlet,* of course. It's an essay entitled 'The First and Last Words of Hamlet', and I don't know how to begin it let alone end it! Would you like a glass of Coke?

GEORGE: Yes please.

[Chief Inspector goes to a little paraffin fridge, fishes out a half empty family-size coke bottle, turns up a glass, and pours. Hands to George, who receives it with gratitude.]

GEORGE: Thank you. *[Drinks thirstily]* That's better. Hamlet, as you know, plays many parts, but his chief role is that of clown.

CHIEF INSPECTOR: Hang on. Do you mind if I take notes? *[Finds pad and pen]*

GEORGE: Not at all. *[Five second pause]* Ready?

CHIEF INSPECTOR: Ready.

GEORGE: He has several characteristics of the typical clown. For ex-ample he is a great punster, a great imitator, a lover of paradoxes…

CHIEF INSPECTOR: And a bachelor.

GEORGE: Indeed. He is closer to the tragi-comic Feste in *Twelfth Night*, than to Iago in *Othello* or Brutus in *Julius Caesar*, though he has something in common with all these. He is Shakespeare's study of the young man; Antony is his study of the middle-aged man; Lear is his study of the old man. Like Feste, Hamlet is a corrupter of words. His famous question —

CHIEF INSPECTOR: 'To be or not to be?'

GEORGE: Indeed. His question is not overtly answered in the play, though it is approached when, towards the end, he says 'let be'.

CHIEF INSPECTOR: May I ask what this has to do with my essay topic?

GEORGE: There's a connection, I think.

CHIEF INSPECTOR: [Pours George more Coke] Go on.

GEORGE: OK, what are Hamlet's first words?

CHIEF INSPECTOR: 'A little more than kin and less than kind'.

GEORGE: Right. He is responding to his uncle/father, Claudius, who, after verbally caressing the son of Polonius ('Take thy fair hour Laertes, time be thine'), turns hesitantly to his nephew/son and says, 'But now my cousin Hamlet, and my son…'. Hamlet's first words are an aside, only the audience hears him. A little more than the word 'kin' is the word 'kind' – one letter more; a little less than the word 'kind' is the word 'kin' – one letter less.

CHIEF INSPECTOR: Not so fast!

GEORGE: [With growing excitement] Sorry, but notice how close both words are, visually and aurally, to 'king'.

CHIEF INSPECTOR: 'The play's the thing'.

GEORGE: Yes, and Zimbabwe's a prison.

CHIEF INSPECTOR: Have some more Coke. [Pours] You were saying.

GEORGE: Hamlet is a little more than kin in that he is nephew and son (and 'cousin'); he is a little less than kind in that he is not as close as a real son.

CHIEF INSPECTOR: He is also hinting that he might be dangerous.

GEORGE: Yes. 'Kind' refers to the station belonging to one by birth. Hamlet feels that he should be king. 'Kind' also refers to a class of the same sex. Hamlet implies that he is not fully male. 'Kind' also means natural. Hamlet …

CHIEF INSPECTOR: Slow down please?

GEORGE: [More slowly] Hamlet suggests that he is unnatural. To do one's kind is to do what is natural, to perform the sexual function. [Five second pause]

CHIEF INSPECTOR: Go on, Mr George; this is most interesting.

GEORGE: It means well bred, well born, gentle; it means affectionate, loving, fond; it means grateful, thankful; it means... Hamlet the solipsist is less than these qualities.

CHIEF INSPECTOR: Solip... what?

GEORGE: Solipsism is the view that the self is all that exists or can be known. I use it to describe Hamlet pejoratively as an egomaniac, like...

CHIEF INSPECTOR: Like?

GEORGE: Like, well...

CHIEF INSPECTOR: Never mind. Have the rest of the Coke. [Pours]

GEORGE: Thank you.

CHIEF INSPECTOR: Go on, please?

GEORGE: If one meaning of '...less than kind' is not fully male, what about '...more than kin'?

CHIEF INSPECTOR: What about it?

GEORGE: The line is antithetical. For every 'more' there should be a 'less'. If you look up the word 'kin' in the OED, you will find that it can mean a crack, chink, or slit; fissure in the earth; crack in the skin. Could it be that when Hamlet says '... a little more than kin', he is saying, at one level, not fully female? [Five second pause]

CHIEF INSPECTOR: Go on.

[Terrible scream from somewhere in the building]

GEORGE: ... Er ... furthermore, the primary meaning of 'kin': family, race, blood relations: is derived from a number of earlier forms, some of the more interesting being 'kunni' (old Swedish), 'chunni' (old High German), 'kunne' (middle Dutch), and 'kuni' (Gothic). Is this one of Hamlet's numerous aural puns? Is he saying, in effect, I am neither male nor female; I am male and female?

CHIEF INSPECTOR: I get your drift, Mr George, but I wonder what the Open University will make of it. I think we've got more than enough material on Hamlet's first words; let us leave his last words for another time, shall we. *[Shouts] Mujeragadhi!* The guard will escort you back to your cell. Pleasant dreams, Mr George.

GEORGE: Thank you, er… *[Door opens, guard escorts George away]*

CURTAIN

Scene 7: *Prison cell, as before plus some laboured snoring and people calling out in their sleep.*

FIRST PRISONER: We kept you some porridge. Sorry it is in my hand.

GEORGE: Thank you but I couldn't eat a thing.

SECOND PRISONER: You are tired. Did they torture you?

GEORGE: No. The Chief Inspector was extremely pleasant to me *[Pause]* – but I don't think he was sincere.

FIRST PRISONER: They hate you because you are white; they hate us because we are Ndebele. They call us dissidents.

SECOND PRISONER: We both lost the war of Independence. You whites are only suffering now, because of MDC; but we Ndebele, we have been suffering since 1980. Look here: what do you see?

GEORGE: Cripes, You've lost a foot!

SECOND PRISONER: That was during Gukurahundi, 1983.

GEORGE: What happened?

SECOND PRISONER: Fifth Brigade. They came to our village, there by Lupane. They say we are dissidents. Even my sister who was only twelve years old. We were asleep when they came. They marched us at gun point until we came to the Cewale River. There were about sixty of us villagers. They beat us for hours. They were using thick branches. Then they lined us up and shot us.

GEORGE: Your sister too?

SECOND PRISONER: Yes. She got a bullet through the head. She was standing next to me. I was lucky. They got me in the foot, and I pretended to be dead. Three others survived because they pretended to be dead. It was not so difficult in the darkness, even though they were

22

walking round finishing us off. The next day they came back to our village looking for survivors, but I was hiding in the bush. My foot went rotten so the doctor at St Luke's hospital had to cut it off.

GEORGE: I'm sorry.

SECOND PRISONER: It was far much worse for old Dhlamini here. His whole family got burnt to death in their hut. Tell him, *umfowethu*.

FIRST PRISONER: No, they were not burnt to death. They were burnt but it was not the fire, it was the bullets. That was in Tsholotsho, I think February 1983... Where were you then, Mabuku?

GEORGE: Why do you call me Mabuku?

FIRST PRISONER: Isn't it, you read books?

GEORGE: Oh, I see. I guess I was safely at home in Bulawayo, reading books. We had no idea what was going on outside of town. Did they really kill your entire family?

FIRST PRISONER: They did. The soldiers came in the morning, about twenty. They rounded us up and locked us in my hut. Not only my family, which was the wife and the baby and the two girls. There were two other men, five other women, two with babies, and some children. They set fire to the hut. I forced the door open, and as we ran out they shot us. I was hit in stomach, and they left me for dead. But I recovered. Look, here is the wound.

GEORGE: It's a terrible scar.

FIRST PRISONER: It was the infection.

GEORGE: Were all the others killed?

FIRST PRISONER: All. I lost everything.

[Whistle]

GUARD: *Chinja, chinja, chinja!*

SECOND PRISONER: Time for sleep.

[Muttering, groaning, whimpering as those who had been lying on their sides stand up and those who had been standing, including George and his two friends, lie down. Cursing from guards.]

GEORGE: This is preposterous! Why don't they release me? They haven't formally charged me with anything.

SECOND PRISONER: They will release you on Monday morning. That is their way. They pick you on Friday and let you go on Monday.

GEORGE: Even if my bail has been paid?

FIRST PRISONER: It is their way.

GEORGE: When will they release you and… er…

SECOND PRISONER: I am Ndiweni.

GEORGE: How do you do? I am George. When will they release you?

SECOND PRISONER: After two years. We have no money for bail.

GEORGE: How much is it?

SECOND PRISONER: Five hundred, five hundred.

GEORGE: I'll try to raise it for you when I get out.

BOTH PRISONERS: *Siyabonga*. We thank you.

VOICE: George!

GEORGE: Yes?

VOICE: Come this way!

GEORGE: Oh no, not again! Excuse me. Sorry. Sorry. *[He battles to extricate himself from the cramped, groaning, sighing bodies. Exits with guard.]*

CURTAIN

Scene 8: *Now late at night. Chief Inspector's room. George and Chief Inspector sit together at table sipping cups of tea.*

CHIEF INSPECTOR: Now let me see. Your last words were, 'I am neither male nor female; I am male and female'.

GEORGE: Where did you learn shorthand?

CHIEF INSPECTOR: I trained as a journalist. I was, for a time, with the BBC World Service. Is your tea sweet enough?

GEORGE: Yes thank you. It's very good.

CHIEF INSPECTOR: You look tired.

GEORGE: I'm exhausted. It's impossible to sleep in the cell.

CHIEF INSPECTOR: Well, I won't keep you much longer. Let's look at Hamlet's last words, shall we?

GEORGE: How do they go?

CHIEF INSPECTOR: 'The rest is silence'.

GEORGE: Then he dies.

CHIEF INSPECTOR: Then he dies.

GEORGE: Whenever death happens in Shakespeare's plays, we look for its antithesis, sex.

CHIEF INSPECTOR: Surely life is the antithesis of death?

GEORGE: Sex is life intensifed.

CHIEF INSPECTOR: [*Not too convinced*] Go on.

GEORGE: Remember the clown in *Antony and Cleopatra*: 'I wish you joy o' the worm'. A colloquial meaning of the word 'dying', familiar to Shakespeare, was 'reaching orgasm', what we today call 'coming', and what the commercially minded Victorians called 'spending'. We shall find our sexual reference in the word 'rest', but let's first look at the word 'silence'. No more casuistry, sophistry, quibbling, declaiming; no more self-deceit, teasing, tormenting, hinting, bewailing; in short: no more words. This is the tragic Hamlet, the melancholic. But what if Hamlet the clown speaks the word in the imperative, directly to the audience, telling them to shut up while he dies on stage: 'The rest is… SILENCE!'? This is the comic Hamlet. Comedy is the antithesis of tragedy; comedy is sex, tragedy is death.

CHIEF INSPECTOR: Ah, so Hamlet is comical and tragical?

GEORGE: Indeed.

CHIEF INSPECTOR: Go on, Mr George. You said we would find our sexual reference in the word 'rest'?

GEORGE: 'Rest' has at least four layers of meaning, and one of them is sex. In *Romeo and Juliet* the nurse advises Juliet to, quote: 'sleep for a week, for the next night (pun on [*spells*] k-n-i-g-h-t), I warrant,/The County Paris hath set up his rest,/That you shall rest but little'. When a lance is in rest it is erect, in the loop that holds it in position for the charge. Sex and death are conflated in Hamlet's final words.

CHIEF INSPECTOR: I see… I see.

GEORGE: Hamlet is echoing the songs of Ophelia and the grave-digger, Gertrude's elegiac description of Ophelia's drowning, which is packed with sexual innuendoes.

CHIEF INSPECTOR: But whose lance is it? Death's or Hamlet's.

GEORGE: There's the rub. Hamlet's first and last words, then, help us formulate a reply to his famous question. It's a simple matter of swopping conjunctions.

CHIEF INSPECTOR: To be and not to be…

GEORGE: That is the answer.

CHIEF INSPECTOR: Well, well, well. I must get this written up and sent off. Thank you for your help, Mr George. May I call you George? I hope we shall meet again one day in more convivial circumstances. I believe someone has stood bail for you, so as soon as you sign an Admission of Guilt form, my subordinates will let you go. Guard! *Mugadhijeri!*

George puts down his tea-cup and slowly stands. The Chief Inspector turns on his music, scene fades with Brenda Fassie singing 'Vulindela'.

FINAL CURTAIN

George stood bail for his two prison friends. This little act of kindness would prolong his life.

4

WABENZI

On his way home, George decided to buy some *nanyute* from C. Gauche (PVT) Ltd. His hen, Harriet, loved the shiny little seeds, which sounded like rain when you poured them into an enamel dish. He parked outside the shop, bought the seeds (plus a packet of moringa powder for himself... why, George?) completely unaware that in sixty seconds, his life would be changed utterly. No terrible beauty for George J. George, though he was wearing his green shirt with matching green socks, and though the shadows of clouds on Robert Mugabe Way were changing by the minute.

He started his Ford, and reversed straight into the left front headlight of a brand new, custom-built Mercedes Benz, which then swerved out of control and crashed into a shop wall, thus damaging its other headlight and its fender. Now George, like all teachers who didn't sell black market products on the side, could not afford to take out fully comprehensive car insurance; he had to settle for the minimum requirement, which was called, somewhat mysteriously, Third Party. What if four, or five, or six uninsured 'parties' are involved in the accident? It didn't apply in George's case because there wasn't even a third party; there were just George and a mistress of none other than the Minister of Child Welfare, Sweets and Biscuits, Comrade Pontius Gonzo.

Things might have been a lot worse – for the vehicles, if not the drivers – if it wasn't for a peculiarity of mistresses of chefs. Here, we have a breed who've been given expensive new cars in exchange for hanky-panky – a peculiarity that has not gone unnoticed by the majority of dirt-poor Zimbabweans, who have to walk or crawl to their destinations – and, whether turning out of their driveways (dangerously fast) or cruising on the open road (dangerously slow), they maintain a speed of not less and not more than 40 kilometres per hour.

When George crashed into Mrs Nyamayakanuna's Merc, the damage would have been considerably more if she had been going any faster than 40 kilometres per hour. So it was that they managed to settle, quite amicably, out of court, as the saying goes. George got to keep what was left of the Ford, Beauticious (for that was the complainant's name), got everything else including George's labour – for the rest of his life.

He needed the job anyway, because, hadn't he been asked to leave Girls and Boys Come Out to Play Secondary School after Speech Night, the school's most prestigious occasion? What had got into him, sitting there on the stage, resplendent, like the other teachers, in his robe and gown, sipping neat Skipper cane spirit from one of those plastic straws, which, owing to a concertinaed section in the middle, could bend in any direction without blocking the searing outflow. He'd managed to conceal the bottle in the folds of his academic gown, but the straw was conspicuous, and so were his efforts to reach it. His Worship the Mayor, distinguished guests, parents and pupils thought he was having a stroke. One of his Form 3 Remove pupils who appeared to be a girl but who bore the ambiguous name of City Lights, actually cried out for all to hear – it was during the headmaster's speech – that Mr George was dying.

Mr George wasn't dying – not quite yet – he was breaking the rules, embarrassing the school, shocking his more sensitive colleagues, sending the entire pupil body into paroxysms of laughter – worst of all, infuriating the Chairman of the Board, a patriotic old boy of the school who had earned colours for rugby and water polo (wasn't his name on one of the boards in the hall – in gold lettering?): R.S.V.P. Labrador-Crack, CEO Sell-Buy (PVT) Ltd.

The following day George had been summoned to the headmaster's office where the entire board of governors was waiting to admonish and then dismiss him. They allowed him to serve out the term because they were not then in a position to replace him – A-Level English teachers were no longer falling out of trees in beleaguered Zimbabwe.

It was while serving his term's notice that the switching of portraits had occurred, followed shortly by his encounter with a motor car so expensive that a few spare parts were worth more than his house and its entire contents. His pension payout, after forty years of full-time service, bought him two jam doughnuts and a soft tomato.

5

LETTING SLIP

Quick to learn from the new farmers, those patriotic sons of the soil who were in the process of expediting the mother of all agricultural seasons, Beauticious gave George forty-eight hours to move from his house (now hers) to his servant's quarters (now hers). He was permitted to take only his clothes and his toothbrush. His three pets would become common property, as long as George cared for them in his free time, between the hours of 8 p.m. and 6 a.m. and Sundays, and as long as they didn't bother Beauticious' own pets: two killer dogs named Hercules and Ajax, which she had purchased from a bankrupt security firm. Well, they didn't bother Hercules and Ajax for long. No need to go into details about feathers, fur, and George's broken heart.

She would pay him the minimum wage and supply him with 5 kilograms of mealie meal per month, and five leaves of spinach or rape per day, depending on availability. She would also hire him out to friends and acquaintances as a driver, at private functions like weddings, funerals and birthdays. In order to make ends meet, George sold his Ford to one of his ex-colleagues, a teacher of Business Management, Accounts, Economics and, at the risk of bathos, History. This teacher bought and sold items such as cooking oil, sugar and washing soap on the black market. He also gave extra lessons to nearly all his pupils at Boys and Girls Come Out to Play Secondary School (since he taught them next to nothing in class) and charged them in foreign currency. For some strange reason neither the parents nor the administration saw anything irregular in this fraudulence. Consequently Mr (Comrade to you!) Gonye could easily afford to purchase George's considerably damaged car. The collision with the Merc had reduced its boot to a mere cubby hole.

With the money from this sale, George bought back from Beauticious, his record player, his records, and most of his books. He had enough left over to buy three months' supply of firewood, which, now that the new owner had begun clearing the garden to plant mealies, was in temporary abundance. Beauticious employed a gardener, a distant relative called Joseph, who did the tree felling and the stumping, and who prepared the ground for the planting and cultivation of Zimbabwe's staple crop. Joseph lived in the wooden tool shed, which George had erected many years before. He shared George's toilet and cold shower facilities, and they frequently cooked and ate together at the open fire, which they built behind the wall of the servant's quarters that gave some protection from the prevailing south easterly winds.

"*Iwe*, George!" (She pronounced it Joji).

"Madam?"

"Buya tata lo ma inja for walks." Beauticious talked to George for the most part in what the Rhodesians called 'Kitchen Kaffir' or 'Fanagalo' or 'Chilapalapa', because that is how she remembered being talked to by white people when she was a little girl. "Hey picannin, haikona bulala lo ma flowers gatina!" Haikona this, haikona that. Both her parents had been domestic workers for the same white family, her father a 'cook boy' and her mother a 'housegirl', and she had grown up in servants' quarters not dissimilar to those that George now lived in.

"Coming, Madam." George left off polishing the windows in the lounge with damp newspaper, and hurried to fetch the dogs' choke chains. This was one of his most dreaded jobs. Hercules and Ajax used their daily walks to terrorise the neighbourhood. They visited every gate, dragging George as if he were no more than an empty tin tied to the rear bumper of a wedding car. 'Cry havoc,' he recalled the words of Marc Antony in *Julius Caesar*, 'and let slip the dogs of war'.

The madam was on her cellphone, car keys in hand, about to make her daily trip to Muscles and Curves where she engaged in physical exercises known as workouts. There she met other *nouveau riche* ladies of all colours (Curves) who were battling to come to terms with the contradiction that the richer you got, the more you had to contend with ennui, nutrient medium for the cultivation of illicit affairs (Muscles). Her children, the twin sons, Helter and Skelter, and the daughter, Ultimate, were at school – George's old school – Boys and Girls Come out to Play. The sons were beginning their A-Levels and the daughter her O-Levels (now called

IGCSE). Fortunately George hadn't taught any of them, so his position in their household was less embarrassing than it might have been. He was fond of the children, and they seemed to be fond of him. Indeed, it perplexed him that such a vulgar, abrasive mother could produce such polite, well-behaved children.

The dogs loved George because he was the only human being who gave them any attention. When they saw him approaching with the leads, whispering "Hush, dogs, hush," they thumped their tails in excitement. They sat still (after all they were trained guard dogs) when he slipped the choke chains over their heads. At first George had found it difficult to forgive Ajax and Hercules for what they had done to his pets, but he reasoned eventually that they were not responsible for what the security firm had turned them into. And it was precisely their viciousness which appealed to Mrs Nyamayakanuna. She wanted to be protected from tsotsis who were increasing in direct proportion to the collapsing Zimbabwean economy, caused, as the madam never failed to remind George, by his kith and kin in England and America. George's kith and kin, what little he knew of them, originated somewhere in Eastern Europe, possibly Lithuania, possibly Estonia, possibly the land of the blood-sucking vampire, Count Dracula (that's enough, George!).

The dogs lurched ahead of George, who kept appealing to them to "Hush, dogs, hush," making terrible gasping sounds as their choke chains tightened. Ajax was a German Shepherd cross Doberman Pinscher, Hercules a German Shepherd cross Rhodesian (the only time this word may be used in a politically correct context) Ridgeback. Some of the embarrassing (and sometimes frightening) things George had to contend with when he 'walked' the dogs was, a) they growled at people on the road, b) they lifted their legs against all the telephone and electricity poles, c) they crapped in private driveways, and d) they fought running battles at the gates of every house he passed, with the dogs on the other side, the dogs with territorial imperative. What George dreaded more than anything else on earth was the unlikely but possible event of an open gate, and this was about to happen.

They were somewhere in Essex Road. George was trying to untangle himself from the choke chains (Hercules had run round him one way,

Ajax the other) when he noticed it, second house on the left. It was one of those sliding electric gates, and it was open because the householder was busy driving out. The driver was none other than ninety-year-old Florence Partridge, Pioneer, self proclaimed Bride of Christ, pet lover, and admirer of the men who created the British Empire, Robert Falcon Scott in particular. She kept by her bedside three books: the Bible (King James), Scott's *Last Expedition*, and Apsley Cherry-Garrard's *The Worst Journey in the World*. She saw Scott as the *beau idéal* of imperialism. In the last days of Rhodesia, a month or two before the arrival, to celebrate independence from colonial rule, of Bob Marley and the Wailers, she had written a letter to the editor of the *Bulawayo Chronicle*, in which she quoted Scott's last words:

I do not think we can hope for any better thing now. We shall stick it out to the end, but we are getting weaker, of course, and the end cannot be far.

It seems a pity, but I do not think I can write more.

R. Scott.

For God's sake look after our people.

The 'our people' in that last despairing line refers to the dependents of Scott and his party back in England but Florence, no mean allegorist, intended it for the fast diminishing (by exodus) white community of the new Zimbabwe.

Electric gates, which cannot be properly maintained because of chronic theft, shortages of spares, shortages of skills, and regular extended power cuts, become deadly hazards. Either they fail to open or close (passive deadly hazard), or they open or close before they are meant to (active deadly hazard). Florence's gate did both. It failed to close when it should have, and closed when it shouldn't have. The result was carnage: three dead pedigree Pekinese dogs, one dead Siamese cat, and one dead bride of Christ. Two of the dogs and the cat were killed by Hercules and Ajax, one dog was crushed by the electric gate, and Florence died of a heart attack, happily it seems, because when she looked out of her side window and saw the fast approaching spectre of George (crying "Hush, dogs, hush!") being pulled along by Hercules and Ajax, her face lit up and she called out – George distinctly heard it – she called out: "Robert Scott, you have stirred the heart of every Englishman." Then her car stalled, and she died. Just like that.

6

A LITTLE TOUCH OF GEORGY
IN THE NIGHT

One Sunday just before bedtime, George was sitting on the step outside his *khaya* enjoying the sweet honey of evening cestrum and the occasional call of a spotted eagle owl, when he received visitors, the twins, Helter and Skelter. They came bearing gifts: a roasted mealie and a sweet potato, ashen from the coals of an open fire. George accepted these gifts graciously and invited the boys to join him in a cup of tea. His fire was still hot enough to boil another pot of water. The boys politely declined this offer but they had a question to ask George. Helter spoke: "What is catharsis?"

George considered this question while gnawing away at his mealie. It had been cooked in its leaves, with a little salt. It was tender and so subtly flavoured that it awakened in George's consciousness a memory of Pueblo Indians, of love-death rituals, of mortals wrestling with gods. George had never been to North America so he must have read it somewhere. Longfellow, perhaps? Something trochaic, anyway.

"Catharsis is one of those words that doesn't quite say what it means."

"But…"

"Like Godot."

"Goddo?"

"Or like epiphanic."

"Epi…?"

"…phanic. I think James Joyce was the first to take it out of its Christian context and apply it to secular creativity: "when the soul of the commonest object seems to us radiant". But I think the word 'soul' there is misleading. If 'catharsis' doesn't quite say what it means, 'soul' doesn't quite mean what it says. Mind you it was Stephen Dedalus who said that, not really Joyce, I suppose. They say there's always an ironic gap between author and persona, but I'm not so sure, really… not so sure." George left off the mealie and took a bite out of the sweet potato. It was the purple-skinned kind, more flavoursome than the white. He chewed it with relish (Keats would have called it 'gusto'). Poor bugger... dying in his own excrement, going out like a frog in a frost. The wood ash on the sweet potato made his teeth squeak.

The boys were becoming agitated. Skelter produced his copy of *King Lear* and held it in front of George's colonial blue eyes, faded in this crepuscular time, not a breeze stirred, to grey, his second favourite colour. "Our teacher wants us to find out if this play has catharsis, but she doesn't tell us what catharsis means."

George gently took the battered edition from the boy and thumbed its pages. "*Othello* must have gone off the syllabus," he said. "That's what I was teaching the A-Level students. This is a tough one."

"It's terrible," said Skelter. "The teacher makes us read it like a play..."

"Well, it is a play."

"Yes, but we don't understand a word of it."

"It's just a noise," said Helter.

"'Blow, winds, and crack your cheeks'."

"Pardon?"

"Noise. Would you like me to read it with you?"

"Would you, George?"

"Of course. But only on Sundays. The rest of the time I'm too exhausted to do anything but sleep."

"Thank you, George – when can we start?"

"Right now, I guess." George stood up painfully. "Let me locate my text. He disappeared into his single room, discovered that his single electric light had blown, realised that his single candle would not provide enough light for his tired old eyes, and returned to the boys who were waiting expectantly on his doorstep. "Sorry boys," he said, "we are going to have to do this during the day. I can't read in this weak light."

"We have torches," said Skelter.

"No, torches won't do; not for me, anyway. Let's talk a bit about the play tonight, and then, next Sunday we can meet sometime during the day."

"After church?"

"That suits me," smiled George who was no churchgoer. "Sit down boys, and let's talk about catharsis."

"Yes please, George." The boys found places to sit on the ground while George resumed his seat on the step. "Our teacher says we must look up Arsenal on the internet."

"Arsenal?"

"Yes. He's the one who wrote about catharsis."

"Oh I see." George resisted a smile. "You must have misheard. Your teacher meant Aristotle. He writes about catharsis in his *Poetics*: 'a tragedy is the imitation of an action that is serious and also, as having magnitude, complete in itself... with incidents arousing pity and fear, wherewith to accomplish its purgation of such emotions.' Catharsis is a purging or cleansing – an emotional release. I'm not sure if Aristotle was referring to the audience or the actors, or both. I think most syllabuses take it to mean audience reaction.

"The question we have to ask ourselves, boys, but only once we've read the play, is: do you and I experience an emotional release when the curtain closes on the final act? Do our feelings of fear (which distance us from Lear) and pity (which draw us closer to Lear), do they merge into a threshold, which is neither fear nor pity, but a third feeling, a paradox..."

"Paradox?"

"It's more than a figure of speech, you know; it's where all thought ends, if you're a philosopher; and where all thought begins, if you're a poet. And they've both got it wrong because, as English teachers know, it's where all thought ends-and-begins, or begins-and-ends. Take this mealie." He raised the half-eaten ear and waved it in front of the boys. "It is the staple food of Zimbabwe; consequently it has accrued a powerful symbolism, like bread in the Bible. It is a synecdoche for sustenance, both physical and spiritual. It is synonymous with our land, our sovereignty. It's the colour green on our flag. But it's a product of biological imperialism. So is the sweet potato. The colonisers introduced it. It has also, therefore, accrued a powerful latent symbolism. It is a synecdoche for oppression, exploitation..."

"That makes it a paradox?" said Helter.

"Yes, in the Zimbabwean context. It is simultaneously good and evil."

"What did we eat before?"

"Small grains: sorghum, rapoko… much healthier, much better suited to our climate."

"But not so tasty."

"Not so tasty."

"My favourite is KFC," said Helter.

"Mine is pizza," said Skelter.

"Mine is smoked salmon on thin slices of rye bread," said George wistfully. "But, to get back to your set work, *King Lear* is possibly Shakespeare's most paradoxical play. The adults behave like children and the children behave like adults. Is the play cathartic? I don't think so. Shakespeare was more of a poet than a dramatist. His denouements are more ambivalent than cathartic. There is always a troubled space between what has happened at the end of the play and what the surviving speakers say. T.S. Eliot called it the consolation of rhetoric. Standing over the bodies of Lear and Cordelia, Albany stupidly says:

> … All friends shall taste
> The wages of their virtue. And all foes
> The cup of their deservings.

And that insufferable moraliser, Edgar, even more stupidly says (and they are the last words of the play):

> The weight of this sad time we must obey,
> Speak what we feel, not what we ought to say.
> The oldest hath borne most; we that are young
> Shall never see so much, nor live so long."

Helter, who had been following the words in his text, said, "It's Albany, not Edgar."

"Oh," replied George, "you must have the quarto version, not the folio. It supports my point that Shakespeare was more interested in poetry than drama."

"But what's wrong with Albany's and Edgar's words?"

"Empty rhetoric. It's what Shakespeare exposes in *Twelfth Night* – are you doing *Twelfth Night?*

"Yes. It's our other Shakespeare."

"Good. They complement each other quite nicely. One is comi-tragic and the other is tragi-comic…"

"Which is which?"

"That I'm not too sure about. It's always dangerous to attempt to classify Shakespeare's plays. He satirises the attempt in *Hamlet* when Polonius says, 'The best actors in the world, either for tragedy, comedy, history, pastoral, pastoral-comical, historical-pastoral, tragical-historical, tragical-comical-historical-pastoral, scene individable, or poem unlimited.' Here Shakespeare's not just having a go at Polonius; he's also having a go at your friend Arsenal… er… Aristotle."

"Excuse me, George" said Helter, "may you go back to 'empty rhetoric'?"

"It's 'will you' not 'may you', my boy; and when you say the word 'rhetoric', you stress the first syllable, as I have just done, not the middle syllable."

"Sorry, Sir."

"Don't say 'sorry', and please don't call me 'Sir'. I forfeited that title some months ago."

"Sorry, Sir."

"Now, to get back to *Twelfth Night*… er… do you remember what Feste says about a sentence?"

"I know that part!" cried Skelter, suddenly animated. "I learned it as a quote."

"Go on."

"Um… 'a sentence is but a chev'ril glove to a good wit - how quickly the wrong side may be turned outward'."

"Good, but what does it mean?"

"I don't know."

"What's a chervil glove?" asked Helter.

"Cheveril. It's kid leather," said George, "soft and flexible. Feste says that a sweet talker can make a sentence mean whatever he wants it to mean."

The three laughed happily together and George complimented the boys on their knowledge. He thought that was a good time to pack it in for the night, and he sent the boys home (for nearly forty years his own family home) with a small task, as preparation for next Sunday's lesson on King Lear: look up the words 'synecdoche' and 'ambivalent', find out about Cinderella, and find three examples of paradoxes, either in life or in literature.

As he turned to go into his room he heard the owl call 'hoo- hoo'. Then its mate replied 'Hoo-oo-hoo'. A spondee and an amphimacer (also known as the cretic foot):

> *Sound the flute*
> *Now it's mute;*
> *Birds delight*
> *Day and night.*

7

FOR SHE MY MIND HATH SO DISPLAC'D

George was an insomniac but, unlike the Macbeths, he enjoyed his habitual sleeplessness. His nocturnal routine seldom varied. If there was enough light he would read (at this time he was revisiting his favourite author, Charles Dickens) until his eyelids grew heavy; then he would take off his glasses and place them carefully under the bed, take a swig of water from his plastic Mazoe Orange bottle, and turn on his wall-facing side. Then he would sink into the arms of Morpheus and dream – such dreams – until about 2 a.m. when his eyes would suddenly open wide. First, he would re-live those parts of his dreams that he could recall; then he would go over the previous day's events as they trickled back into his consciousness; finally he would drift into a suspended state between sleeping and waking where, for one or two hours, he would gently hallucinate. He loved those hours of wakefulness and semi-wakefulness because they seemed to slow down time, gave him a sense of being in the eternal present. Then Wilhelmine came (bliss), and went (torment), and his recollections of their brief time together invaded the blessed numbness of his insomnia with the pain of loss.

Wilhelmine was German, part of a wave of NGOs from the so-called First World who, ever since Independence in 1980, had been breaking with salty promise on the landlocked shores of Zimbabwe. She wanted to refine her English, and someone had recommended George. Wilhelmine had a pretty face, but behind it stretched a head so wide and a nose so flat-hooked that, combined with long skinny legs, a predilection for the colour green, and simply no bum, she resembled a grasshopper, the edible kind, which the Ndebele call *intethe*. She was young, far too young for George, now in his early sixties; and she warned him; right from the start she warned him, in metaphor, in parable, in the words of her favourite poet, Hermann Hesse, that all he could expect from her was a moment, just a

39

moment, of fulfillment. What did she call it? *Stufen*. "We should move on, step by step," she advised him (when he began to cling to her), paraphrasing the poem of that title, "and we should be cheerful about it."

"But…"

"As soon as we are used to our surrounding and feel contented, the danger of inertia is there. Don't you see that, George?"

"I…"

"Only those who are willing to make a new start escape complacency."

"This is simply how the dumpers console the dumped."

"Bitte?"

"Nothing. It's just that…"

With the aid of Collins German dictionary George had struggled through Hesse's poem and was surprised at *its* complacency. He recalled the same message in an earlier Romantic, William Blake:

> *He who binds to himself a joy*
> *Doth the wingéd life destroy;*
> *He who kisses the joy as it flies,*
> *Lives in eternity's sunrise.*

"'*Que voulez-vous, Monsieur? C'est les mots; on' n'a rien d'autre.*' Now there's consolation! Good old crease-faced Beckett!"

George turned over and felt for his water bottle. He knocked it over, and because he had failed to secure the click-down lid, half its contents were spilled on the cement floor. He cursed mildly, took a swig, secured the lid, and put the bottle back on the floor. Then he turned back to the wall.

Now where was I? Oh yes, Wilhelmine (subject of George's never-to-be-revealed Petrarchan sonnets). They were to meet once a week, Sunday mornings as it turned out, for what Mina (George's choice of diminutive) called conversational English. They sat in the dining room, at the small Oregon pine table, (which Beauticious has since replaced with a very large Formica table), Mina at the head and George to her left. Occasionally their knees touched. On their first day, Mina wore a white shirt and a grasshopper green ankle-length skirt. Like most Germans of her generation she kept her hair very short, a schoolboy cut. Her skin was as white as endpaper and she wore African beads around her neck. Her face was covered in freckles; even her green eyes were freckled.

She greeted him with a lovely smile: "Sorry I am coming late, George, but the police were stopping people for licence checks."

Ah, thought George, the present participle. Let the lesson commence. "Er… hullo, Mina. No problem. There are no clocks in the forest."

"What?"

"The weekend (weakened), you know. Holiday. Time does not matter." He motioned her into the house and pulled back her chair. She automatically dusted the seat with her hand before sitting down.

"Why are you stating the forest?"

"It's a quotation from Shakespeare's play, *As You Like It*."

"But why a forest, George?" She smiled quizzically at him, and his stomach flipped.

"It's a place where you escape from Everyday, from linear time; you know, tick-tock-tick-tock…"

"Forests are sweet when the world does not enter them. That's an Indian saying."

"Yes, the same idea."

"But in German folklore the forest is a place to fear, a place where little children are getting lost."

"Like Little Red Riding Hood?"

"Yes, and like…"

"Tom Thumb?"

"I was going to say *Hänsel und Gretel*."

"Them too. The forest terrifies us, according to Jung, because it may reveal what we suppress in our unconscious existence. Would you like a cup of tea, Mina?"

"No tea, thank you, George."

"I'm sorry I don't have any coffee."

"That's OK. A glass of water would be nice."

George poured his student a glass of water and then sat down next to her. "Shall we begin?"

"Yes, but first you must say how much you are charging."

"No charge, Mina, it's a pleasure."

"Then we can't continue on."

Ah, thought George, prepositions. Next lesson. "I really don't know what to charge; I have no idea what my time is worth; not very much if you go by teachers' salaries." He paused to ponder the issue. "I tell you what, Mina, you can pay me in kind."

She looked at him from lowered eyebrows and said, teasingly, "Are you meaning sex?"

George blushed to the roots of his thinning grey hair. "No, no… of course not. I… er… I was thinking of, maybe, say, a bottle of local wine for every… er… four lessons."

"Red or white?"

"White, please."

"Sweet or dry?"

"Sweet, Please."

"You have got yourself a bargain, George," smiled Wilhelmine.

"Deal. Not bargain. Deal."

She smiled. "Our lessons have begun. You have got yourself a deal."

George was beginning to think that Mina was the prettiest girl he had ever conversed with. He was aware of a quickening pulse rate, and his voice quavered slightly when he spoke. "Shall we start with the present participle?"

"Mit klopfenden Herzen."

"Sorry?"

"With beating heart."

George blushed again. "Oh, I get it: the present participle."

"In German we add -d to the infinitive form."

"In English we add –ing."

"I know."

"You see, there is a tendency for second language speakers to use the present participle in all three tenses: past, present and future. As it's an imperfect verb you can get away with this, but it sounds clumsy."

"For example… George?"

"Well, when you arrived, you said, 'I am coming late.'" For some reason George began to blush again. Wilhelmina sipped her water and looked at him without moving her head. "You should have said, 'I'm late'."

"Well, I was apologising..." She grinned at him.

"So you get the point. Avoid the present continuous if you can. And yet, poetically, it is the most effective of all the tenses."

"Why is that?" She shifted slightly and her left knee brushed against George's right knee.

George kept as still as his chair. He swallowed, became acutely aware of the movement of his Adam's apple, wondered if there were any hairs sticking out of his nostrils, automatically rubbed his nose, and then began. "It has paradoxical qualities. It has the action of a verb as well as the in-action of an adjective (and, in our world of grammatical laxity, a noun). Furthermore, since it can be used in all the tenses, past present and future, it has the effect of merging time. What did Bergson call it...?"

A cock-crow jolted George out of his reverie and he turned onto his stomach, burying his face in the musty down of his pillow. Because of a sore back, the lumbar region, he could not lie in that position for too long. It was the next-door neighbours' son's Japanese bantam: a snowy white bird who answered to the name of Toyoto. He and his concubine sometimes visited George through a hole in the fence next to George's *khaya*. At least they did until Hercules and Ajax moved in. Cocks all over the neighbourhood began responding to Toyota's challenge; then a dog began barking, which activated an entire orchestra of dogs. There were yaps, growls, howls, and whimpers. Somewhere a car alarm went off, and it was only when that terrible racket stopped that George was able to resume his recalled lesson with she who had so displaced his mind.

"Now where was I? Oh yes. 'Duration.' Take the word 'setting', Mina..."

"You and me are setting down?"

"No, that's 'sitting'. And it's 'I', not 'me'. 'Setting' is a present participle with multiple paradoxical effects. Consider Wordsworth's use of it in one of his greatest poems, 'Lines Composed a Few Miles Above Tintern Abbey'. I'll see if I can remember the lines. Er...

> *And I have felt*
> *A presence that disturbs me with the joy*
> *Of elevated thoughts; a sense sublime*
> *Of something far more deeply interfused,*

Whose dwelling is the light of setting suns…

"First of all, the sun doesn't set, the world turns. Then, because of its versatility, not always strictly grammatical, I concede, the present participle is the best tense to evoke the eternal present, which is a sort of time-lessness, a merging of past, present, and future. Thirdly, 'setting' functions as a verb and an adjective (or gerundive); so you have movement in stillness. Next, from a lexical point of view, 'setting' means moving, as in 'we were setting out on a journey' or not moving, as in 'the jeweller was setting the diamond in the ring'.

"There's more, and still more. In Wordsworth's poem, the image that emerges from the word 'setting' is of twilight, a moment when light and dark merge. Light symbolises life while dark symbolises death. When these opposites merge, not only in the word but in the image, you get what Keats called the feel of not to feel, or what James Joyce called an epiphany. Wordsworth's own word for it is 'joy'. In truth, the feeling or sensation, or whatever, cannot be explained. It's ineffable.

"Another effect of the present participle is verisimilitude."

"Very-?"

"-similitude. The appearance of being real. The present participle makes it seem to be happening as you read. It draws the reader into the text. Art metamorphoses into life. It's an illusion, of course. But, as Keats said, 'Beauty is truth, truth beauty' …"

"Slow down George, you lose me!"

"Losing me. You are losing me."

"But you said…"

"Oh cripes, the participle. It's not always wrong, you know. The present continuous… ah forget it…"

"George, I invite you to a braai at my place."

Unrequited love. Poor Pip… poor old Joe… poor Tom… poor forked animal… poor… George began to snore gently as he drifted off to sleep, dimly aware of a Heuglin's robin summoning the dawn.

8

A HARD DAY'S NIGHT

George's duties as a domestic worker began promptly at 6 a.m., or sparrow fart in the local idiom. The madam expected, nay demanded, her coffee, white with six sugars, and a plate of *vetkoek*. The ritual was for George to place the tray on the carpet outside madam's bedroom door, knock gently and say, "Coffee, Madam!" Then he would tiptoe back to the kitchen and start preparing breakfast for the family: the three children and Beauticious, and, occasionally, the Minister of Child Welfare, Sweets and Biscuits. George quite liked the Minister because he always tipped him with a middle-of-the-range bearer's cheque. "Yes, *umfaan*," he would say, "go buy yourself some laces for your tackies."

"Don't spoil the boy!" Beauticious would retort. The Minister would chuckle and take another bite of his Colcom pork sausage with scrambled egg and baked beans. "Joji, more coffee for the boss; and enza lo ma toast, checha!"

"Yes, Madam."

In the early days of his servitude George spent much of his life feeling mortified. The chipped enamel tin mug for his fifteen-minute mid-morning left-over coffee break, which he shared with Joseph, sitting on upturned wooden crates in the back yard outside the kitchen door, was bad enough; so was the forty-minute lunch break with its thick slice of yesterday's bread (when available), and mixed fruit jam, washed down with tea dregs; but worst of all was the uniform Beauticious compelled him to wear. Gone were the powder blue safari-suits of his school-teaching days; gone were his light brown Grasshoppers, with socks from Woolworths; gone (Oh dear, George) was his beloved floppy hat, which he wore to umpire inter-school cricket matches. Beauticious made him wear khaki shirt and shorts, the former much too small, the latter much too large. His head-wear was a tasselled red fez while his footwear was white tackies (though Beauticious didn't mind if he went barefoot). But time heals as it destroys, and habit, time's cicatrice, had inured George to the shame of his new role. After all, wasn't it Nell in *Endgame* who said 'nothing is funnier than unhappiness'? And when George caught his reflection in one of the madam's many mirrors scattered about the house, he had to smile.

"Ipi lo toast, Joji? Lo boss yena funa hamba sebenza. Aziko time!"

"Sorry Madam, the power has just gone. I'll have to use the outside fire."

"No ZESA, no fuel, no food. Who is responsible, Joji?"

All five faces at the Formica table looked at him expectantly. "We are, Madam: the British, the Europeans, the Americans."

"You have raped our country barren, Joji. First our women and girls, next our motherland. Shame on you." The Minister clicked his tongue in sympathy.

"Sorry, Madam."

"Sorry? What is sorry? It is too late for that word, Joji. By the way, have you been helping yourself to my sugar?"

"No Madam, I…"

"Basop, wena!"

"Sorry… I mean… shall I do the toast on the outside fire?"

"Yes, and be quick about it. Checha, checha! Fuga steam, Joji!"

Beauticious was just one of the Minister's numerous mistresses. He kept a lady in all the major towns of Zimbabwe, set up in what is quaintly known as small houses. His big house, a mansion on several sprawling acres of prime land in Harare's Borrowdale suburb, was occupied by his wife and his seven legitimate children. The Minister, like all men of great power in Africa (and the world for that matter) had broadcast his seed far and wide. Recently he had been venturing, incognito, into the NGO world. Fruitful pickings there, he had been advised by the boys in his recently (and unfairly) relegated football team, the Black Bustards. Go to the Zambesi Bar, they advised him, and feed your mamba till it regurgitates. The Germans are the easiest; it helps them deal with their Nazi complexes. Why, one *intombi* took on the entire football team as well as the coach. Just ask for *intethe*.

Beauticious was the Minister's favourite; hence the custom-built Mercedes Benz, the immediate cause of George's downfall. Only his wife,

Cushion, did better in the vehicle department, terrorising the cyclists and pedestrians of Harare in her beetle black Hummer with mounted machine gun and a place to hold a can of Coke. All his other mistresses, those he had set up in small houses in Mutare, Masvingo, Gweru, Gwanda, and Kwe Kwe, drove Mitsubishi Pajeros – all at 40 kilometres per hour.

It was time for the children to leave for school, and George handed them their packed lunches, which he had prepared before breakfast. To supplement this wholesome food, their mother gave them, every school day, the equivalent of George's monthly wage to spend on junk at the tuck shop. George rather enjoyed driving the children to and from school. It took him away, briefly, from the drudgery of never-ending household chores, though he was always fearful of being seen by one of his erstwhile colleagues, to hear one of them crow 'how are the mighty fallen' (even though they didn't read the Bible) or 'here comes Johnny head-in-air' (even though they had never heard of Wilhelm Busch).

Breakfast over at last, George washed the dishes (once his property) while Beauticious let her man out of the gate where his chauffer waited for him in a silver-grey Rolls Royce. They waved goodbye to each other, both with cellphones stuck to the sides of their heads like cancerous outgrowths. The Minister was on his way to Gwanda to give support (Parliamentary elections were looming) to the Minister of Medium to Small to Tiny Business Enterprises who was opening a Chinese built, Chinese owned, Chinese food-processing factory. Beauticious was chatting to her best friend, Titty, and inviting her over to tea (she loved to parade George in front of her friends), while the Minister was chatting to his Gwanda mistress, Copacabana, and making sure that she would be available for him while he was in her neck of the woods, so to speak.

After washing the breakfast things and leaving them to dry on the rack and on the sink, George turned to the extremely arduous task of doing the laundry. There was no washing-machine so it all had to be done manually using bars of smelly blue or yellow soap. George's hands, now hard as the spines of leathern Bibles, had suffered terribly in the first weeks of washing, rinsing, and ironing the family's clothes and linen. He would soak a load in the Zinc bath, then item by item (the madam's scarlet and black thongs shocked him) he would apply soap and then scrub them on a ribbed wooden board until all dirt and nearly all stains had been removed. Then he would rinse the soap out of them, and hang them on the clothes-line to dry. He used an assortment of plastic and wooden clothes-pegs to keep them from falling to the ground. Hercules and Ajax, since there was nothing to kill, would keep him company.

So would the birds, the doves in particular. The laughing kind were resident; the red-eyed turtle kind were occasional visitors. George couldn't get over the way they walked so that their heads bobbed like the cork floats he used as a boy, fishing for bream and barbel at Mtshelele Dam in the Matopos, his favourite spot in the world (what world, George?). He had a tendency to anthropomorphise animals, so he worried that the continuous bobbing might give the birds headaches. He attempted to remedy this by dissolving a few grains of aspirin in the bird bath every morning. Not being Doctor Dolittle, he couldn't ask the creatures if their headaches had eased, but judging by their amorous behaviour towards each other and their aggressive behaviour towards other species, not to mention their voracious appetites, he was optimistic.

It wasn't the doves that attracted his attention this morning at the washing line; rather it was the antics of a fork-tailed drongo, the only bird in George's experience that could actually say 'Tweet, tweet'. The drongo was perched in one of the few remaining trees in the garden, an Acacia erioloba, which George had germinated from a seed. He recalled pocketing that seed on a camping holiday to Hwange National Park, more than thirty years before (but where, George, where, are the snows of yesteryear?). Below the drongo several African hoopoes ambled about poking their beaks into the ground. Whenever one came up with a worm, the drongo would swoop and take the morsel straight from the hapless hoopoe's beak. George wondered how the late Florence Partridge might have allegorised this event.

While the washing flapped at his ears and the doves flapped at his feet; while Hercules and Ajax gazed at him with adoring eyes, George sang a medley of songs, songs he'd heard his father sing, and his grandfather before that, and his great-grandmother before that.

> *Just a song at twilight, when the lights are low,*
> *And the flick'ring shadows softly come and go;*

> *Though the heart be weary, sad the day and long,*
> *Still to us at twilight, comes love's old song,*
> *Comes love's o-*

"*Iwe*, Joji!"

"Madam?"

"*Haikona wena iswili mina, Joji?*"

"Sorry, Madam."

"*Buya lapa, checha. Lo Missis Titty yena enza visiting lapa gamina. Tina funa lo ma tea na lo ma keks, iswili?*"

"Yes Madam, mina… er…I'm coming."

George took the peg out of his mouth and used it to secure on the wash line a scarlet thong, as small as David's sling. Then he wiped his hands on his apron and hurried in to the house. The power was back, so he could use the electric kettle. There were two brands of tea in the grocery cupboard: Five Roses for the Madam and Fresh Leaves (in truth, stalks) Tea for the servants. Fortunately he had baked a batch of cupcakes the day before, so he wouldn't have to undergo the humiliation of being shouted at in front of a guest. Despite the shortages of groceries in the country, and the shops being virtually empty, Beauticious presided over a pantry that was laden with the choicest of goods, and a deep-freeze which was packed with the best cuts of super grade beef, pork, lamb, and goat; and a dozen plump chickens; and, and, and… How did she do it? Connections. Let's leave it at that, shall we?

Beauticious liked to use her… well, George's maternal grandmother's… silver tea set, when she had guests. Again fortunately, George had recently polished the items, tray included, and had washed and carefully ironed the beaded lace doilies; so he had high expectations of a little praise.

He was not disappointed. *Inkosikazi* Titty, speaking simultaneously to her cellphone and to Beauticious, nevertheless gave him a brilliant smile when he handed her a cup of tea with milk and six sugars, and a plate of cupcakes decorated with white icing and hundreds and thousands in five bright colours. The television set was on (it was on all the time) featuring some mid-morning American soap opera. The sound was down, however; instead an elaborate music centre leaked from one of its multiple vents, a strangled voice going on nostalgically about all the girls he'd loved.

"That will do, George, thank you," said Beauticious after he had handed her tea and cake.

"Thank you, Madam." He backed out of the dangerously over-furnished lounge wringing his hands and taking extra care not to knock anything over. Then he waited anxiously in the kitchen for the inevitable:

"Joji, futi tea!"

On their way home from school (in the Madam's second car, a Toyota Hilux double-cab) Ultimate began to complain about all the homework she had been given: maths, geography, history, biology, and English. George was concentrating on avoiding the new potholes that had formed since the rains had begun, rains that heralded the mother of all agricultural seasons. Traffic was heavy during the lunch hour, so swerving and weaving was dangerous. But he always kept a sympathetic ear open for the children, and he picked up the note of distress in Ultimate's voice. One of her braids had worked loose and was dangling over her right eye. Or was it her left eye? George couldn't be sure looking at her reflection in the rear-view mirror. He asked her what she had been given for English. It was a *Macbeth* contextual. They had to discuss the appropriateness of the opening scene.

"Did you know that the witches speak in trochaic tetrameters?"

"I beg yours?"

"You know, strong-weak, strong-weak, strong-weak, strong."

"What?"

"The metre is incomplete. Catalectic. The final weak syllable is missing"

Ultimate frowned and looked at her brothers for support. She put her forefinger to her temple and made circular motions with it, thus suggesting that George was out of his mind.

But her brothers would have none of it. "Why don't you ask George to help you with your homework?" said Helter. "Don't forget he was once an English teacher."

"But I don't know what he's talking about." She brushed the braid off her face; it soon returned, swinging slightly like an insufficiently weighted pendulum.

"He'll explain. He's good at explaining. Ask him."

"Would you, George?"

"Of course! When is your homework due?"

"First thing tomorrow morning. Mr Sibanda is very strict."

"Oops, well… that's going to make it a little difficult. But we can talk in the kitchen if you like; while I'm preparing supper."

Ultimate's face brightened. "Great! We can help each other. I'll peel the potatoes."

"And I'll explain the paradoxes."

"Look out!" cried the twins in unison. George swerved to avoid a pot-hole that would have broken the Toyota's suspension. He nearly collided with an oncoming car, which hooted at him and kept on hooting until it was out of hearing. They were all relieved to get home in one piece.

Early that morning George had taken out a chicken to defrost, and he had dried a couple of slices of bread for the stuffing. Ultimate joined him in the kitchen with her copy of *Macbeth*. "What can I do, George?" she asked. She had managed to return the errant braid to its allotted place, and she was all smiles.

"Why don't you prepare the vegetables, Miss Ultimate. There are those potatoes and those carrots to peel, and those lovely young green beans to top and tail. Meanwhile I'll prepare the stuffing for the chicken…"

"Yummy, I love stuffing. What shall I use to peel with?"

George gave her an instrument for stripping the skin off vegetables, and showed her how to use it. Now let's talk about that scene. How does it begin?"

"Hang on." She opened her text and found the place:

ULTIMATE: When shall we three meet again,

GEORGE: In thunder, lightning, or in rain?

ULTIMATE: When the hurlyburly's done,

GEORGE: When the battle's lost and won.

ULTIMATE: That will be ere the set of sun.

ULTIMATE: Where the place?

GEORGE: Upon the heath.

ULTIMATE: There to meet with Macbeth.

GEORGE: I come, Graymalkin!

ULTIMATE: Paddock calls.

GEORGE: Anon!

TOGETHER: Fair is foul, and foul is fair:

Hover through the fog and filthy air.

Ultimate beamed. "How can you say all that without looking at the page?"

"I was an English teacher."

Ultimate sensed that it would be less than tactful to pursue this line, so she said, "Which vegetable shall I start with?"

"Suit yourself. You've got yellow, green, and white. My mother always said that a complete meal should include those three colours. Can you think of another combination?"

"Yes… wait a bit… what about… um… pumpkin… um… rice…"

"And?"

"And… spinach!" She smiled happily.

"That's it! Well done! Now, how many witches are there?"

"She started on the potatoes. "Three. Like the three vegetables?"

"Yes, but the only thing they've got in common is the number three, and that's the first important point to make about this scene."

"Why, George?"

"Because, Miss Ultimate, the number three is a universal symbol of good, or at least of order; and *Macbeth* is a play about the conflict between order and chaos (or disorder)."

"Our teacher said it's about good versus evil."

"That's a more subjective way of putting it." Ultimate frowned so he added, "You could see good as order and evil as chaos."

Ultimate relaxed her frown. "But don't the witches represent evil?"

"Yes."

"Then why are there three if three is a good number?"

"That's the point: the devil can assume a pleasing shape. The witches have appropriated the Trinity." While he talked George squeezed a tube of sausage meat into a bowl. He reduced the dried bread slices to crumbs and added them to the meat. Then he selected an egg from the fridge and plopped it into a jug of water.

"Why are you doing that with the egg?" asked Ultimate who was on her third potato.

"To see if it's fresh. If it floats it is stale; if it sinks it is fresh. In the olden days that's how they tested women to see if they were witches."

"That's not true, George!"

"It is. If a woman was accused of witchcraft she was thrown into the river. If she floated she was guilty; if she sank, she was innocent."

"So if she was innocent she drowned?"

"I'm afraid so. Either way the poor woman lost out. If she didn't drown, they burned her at the stake."

"That's so unfair!"

"It is. Life is unfair." (Easy, George, easy.) Expertly he cracked the egg and, with one hand, emptied it into the bowl.

Ultimate, watching, was impressed: "I have to use both hands."

"It takes a little practice." He added some dried parsley and sage, some finely chopped onion and garlic, and a squeeze of lemon juice. Ultimate was fascinated by the way he used his fingers as a strainer. Finally he added salt and ground pepper. "Ground black pepper is useful if there are weevils in the food. It camouflages them."

"Yuk, that's gross, George!"

"It is, isn't it?" He used a fork to mix the ingredients, and then he checked to see if the chicken was sufficiently defrosted. The giblets, neck, and feet were in a separate plastic bag inside the bird. He gave a foot each to the dogs, chopped the giblets and mixed them in with the stuffing. He thought about stealing the neck for himself but decided against it. Beauticious missed nothing. "How are you getting on with the spud-bashing?"

"Spud-bashing?"

"Peeling the potatoes. It's slang."

"I'm on my fourth."

"Good. Now let's get back to your homework. Notice the first line of the play begins with a question. That's good drama. It creates anticipation in the audience. Notice too that, though the play is entitled *Macbeth*, and focuses on the character of that name, we don't see him in the opening scene."

"He gets mentioned."

"Yes, he gets mentioned, but we don't actually see him before scene 3. That's also good drama."

"Because the audience can't wait to see him?"

"Yes. Expectation, anticipation, suspense… Notice the setting: thunder and lightning, 'an open place'. The chaotic background is appropriate for these bringers of chaos. That's a kind of metaphor known as the objective correlative. If the setting is personified in any way you can call it the pathetic fallacy. All these words!"

Ultimate had moved on to the carrots. "I won't remember any of this for my assignment."

"Yes you will. Enough." George was stuffing the chicken, front and back, with his fingers. When it was done he sealed off the back by tucking the ends of the drumsticks into a flap of skin just below the parson's nose. The front was trickier. Ultimate's eyes boggled like cotton reels as she witnessed George actually putting stitches in the skin with a needle and thread.

"Can I help you in the kitchen more often, George?"

"You can, and you may, Miss Ultimate. Now, the finishing touch." He fetched some rashers of fatty bacon from the fridge and draped them over the bird. Carefully he placed it in a clay roaster (with the politically incorrect RHOASTER stamped on the lid), and then turned to the girl: "Would you like to put it in the oven?"

"OK, but won't I get burnt?"

"Not if you aren't a witch." They both laughed. George made her put on the oven gloves, and talked her through the process. "Careful, the oven is preheated to 180 degrees. Well done! Now you can tell your mother and your brothers that you helped prepare tonight's dinner."

"Mom's still at the gym and my brothers are glued to the TV."

"Well, you finish the carrots and I'll do the beans."

"You said you would explain the paradoxes in this scene."

"Oh yes. Well, we've already discussed the first one. The witches are wicked but they appear to be good because there are three of them. 'Appear' is the key word. The entire play, like all Shakespeare's plays, is about appearance versus reality or art versus nature. The second paradox is the line, 'When the battle's lost and won'. Can you see why?"

"You can't lose *and* win a battle."

"In a sense, you can. Macbeth won the battle for Scotland and lost the battle for his soul. Have you heard of a pyrrhic victory?"

"No."

"Go and fetch your dictionary and we'll look it up." While she was out of the kitchen George quickly washed the potatoes and put them in a pot of water, ready for boiling; then he returned to topping and tailing the beans.

She came back slightly breathless, clutching the Concise Oxford Dictionary, Ninth Edition. This had been one of George's books, which Beauticious had refused to re-sell to him. "How do you spell it?"

"Eye, tea."

"No man, George man," she giggled, "Pyrrhic."

"Pea, why, are, are, aitch, eye, sea."

She soon found the word and read out the definition: " '(Of a victory) won at too great a cost to be of use to the victor, (from the name of Pyrrhus of Epirus, who defeated the Romans at Asculum in 279 BC, but sustained heavy losses)."

"There you are!"

"But look, George, here's another entry for 'pyrrhic': 'a metrical foot of two short or unaccented syllables…'"

"The opposite of a spondee. Let's see if we can find any pyrrhics in your opening scene… er… the second line, 'or in'? What about…"

" 'ere the'?"

"Possibly. Yes. Well done, my girl… I mean, Miss Ultimate. You learn quickly."

"I came first in class last term."

"I know that. We are all very proud of you."

"Are there any other paradoxes? I've got to go and write this thing up."

"The most important paradox of all; the focus of the entire play: 'fair is foul and foul is fair'. The witches are foul in appearance but their equivocations are in a sense fair, because Macbeth and Banquo are allowed to make their own choices. Lady Macbeth is fair in appearance but foul behind the scenes. Cawdor did a foul deed when he betrayed Scotland, but he died fair: 'Nothing in his life / became him like the leaving it'… and so on."

"What did you mean, in the car, by 'strong-weak, strong-weak, strong-weak'?"

"Oh that! Metre. The witches speak in an opposite rhythm to the human characters, but let's leave that for another time. My chores are piling up."

"Thanks, George. Is there anything else I can do in the kitchen?"

George smiled. "No thank you, my dear. You've been a great help to me. Better go and do your homework before it's too late."

She skipped all the way to her bedroom. George returned to his duties, which would keep him going until knock-off time at 8 p.m. – feed the animals, polish the shoes, finish the ironing, scrub the kitchen floor, serve dinner to the family, fold down the bedding…

PARP- PARP. PARP-PARP. PARP-PARP.

The madam was back from gym. Was Joseph around to open the gate, or would he have to run for it?

PARP-PARP. PARP-PARP. PARRRRRRRP!

9

DEUS EX MACHINA

Joseph knocked off earlier than George so if he wasn't away drinking with his friends, he could be relied upon, most nights, to make a fire, and get the sadza going. George, exhausted to the point of collapse, joined him at the fire. His portable wooden crate was already in position. He and Joseph exchanged greetings. George settled his worn-out body on the upturned crate and listlessly watched Joseph stirring porridge with a long wooden spoon. He felt another nasty twinge in his gut. They occurred more regularly these days, but they passed and he chose to ignore them. Reaching into the capacious pocket of his khaki shorts, he withdrew a small cabbage-leaf parcel. In it were the scrapings of four dinner plates: the bones of a chicken (those which had not been fed to the dogs), half a potato, two pieces of carrot, and several green beans. Sadly not a single crumb of stuffing had survived the voracious appetites of the four Nya-mayakanunas. But its mouth-watering scent remained on the scraps.

Next to the sadza pot was a smaller pot, which George and Joseph used to make relish. The pots were supported by a wire grid, which was in turn supported by two cement breeze bricks on opposite sides of the fire. The smaller pot was half filled with merrily boiling water, and into this George tipped the leftovers. The cabbage leaf went in too, piece by torn piece. He felt in his shirt pocket and withdrew a paper pellet. He held it over the relish pot and shook out a mixture of salt and ground pepper. Then Joseph made his contribution, a ripe bird's-eye chilli from a bush growing next to his shack. The gallimaufry began to give off a distinctly pleasant aroma, and George felt his appetite awakening.

The houseboy and the garden boy made desultory conversation while their supper was cooking. George moved his box to the other side of the fire so that he could watch the moon rising, 'with how sad steps'. It used to bleed copper through the tangled branches of a monkey thorn tree, but that tree had recently succumbed to the demands of maize, already beginning to tassel… a divinity killed and planted to become the food of man. Recalling the legend of Mondawmin, was it? George tried to metamorphose, in his imagination, a mealie stalk. Turning Wilhelmine into a grasshopper was easy by comparison. He would need help. He remembered reading about the legend in Longfellow's poem but he didn't have a copy. He did, however, have several of Joseph Campbell's books, and as Campbell had been a world authority on Native American mythology, there was bound to be a version of it somewhere. Not now, though; there was insufficient light for reading even with such a full moon.

George had been half-listening to Joseph's complaints, about Beauticious, about the economy in general, and about the political situation. Joseph was a Karanga from the Zaka district of Masvingo. For years he had been an ardent supporter of Robert Mugabe and ZANU PF, but now he wasn't so sure. For years he had denied Gukurahundi, the massacre by Mugabe's Fifth Brigade of thousands of rural Ndebele, but now he wasn't so sure. For years he believed that the whites were responsible for all Zimbabwe's woes, but now he wasn't so sure. It was from his tribe that Ian Smith had recruited the bulk of the soldiers, which were known as the R.A.R. (previously the K.A.R.), who fought for the Rhodesians against the Freedom Fighters, ZANLA based in Mozambique, and ZIPRA based in Zambia. For years Joseph had been ashamed of this fact, but now he wasn't so sure.

"Let's eat, Joseph," said George, "is the sadza ready?"

"It is ready."

George stood up painfully and went into his room to fetch plates and tea things. The only utensils they needed were their fingers and a spoon for the relish. Joseph took the plates and dished out a generous helping of stiff porridge for both of them. Then he took the relish off the fire and placed it on the ground between them. He mashed the potato and the carrots and the beans, and stirred them into the liquid. The men washed their hands at the tap and then used their fingers to knead the sadza into little balls, which they dipped and scooped in the relish. George took his first bite and was pleasantly shocked by the double heat: temperature and chilli. He had to take in little allotments of breath to help cool things down. Joseph was more resilient.

The liquid in the pot was soon gone but those enticing bones remained. Joseph stared at them. "Do you want them or don't you?" said George, "they're yours." (Joseph makes a dart at the bones, picks them up and begins to gnaw them.) "Tasty?"

"Very." (He resumes his gnawing.)

"I'll get some tea going." George took the relish pot and rinsed it at the outside tap. He filled it with water and returned it to the fire, which Joseph had been stoking. "Where's the lid? It boils more quickly."

JOSEPH: That is better. (He puts what's left of the bones in his pocket.)

GEORGE: That's about what the English say after their first sip of tea.

JOSEPH: What are they saying?

GEORGE: That's better.

JOSEPH: Where is the pot lid?

GEORGE: I don't know. Didn't you have it when you started the relish?

JOSEPH: I was not seeing it then.

GEORGE: It must be around somewhere.

JOSEPH: Sure.

GEORGE: It'll turn up.

JOSEPH: Maybe.

GEORGE: It will, I'm sure.

JOSEPH: Shall we look for it?

GEORGE: Yes, let's look for it.

They do not move.

A vesper bat, and then another, swooped for an insect just above Joseph's head. He ducked and muttered "Muremwaremwa." The dogs, who had been sharing the warmth of the fire, suddenly began to growl.

"Hush boys, hush," said George, and they thumped their tails in the dirt. Then they growled again, ears cocked, muzzles pointed in the direction of the side gate. Simultaneously they jumped up and rushed, barking, in that direction. "Looks like we've got visitors," said George. What's the Ndebele word?"

"*Izithekeli.*"

"No, for bat."

"Bat?"

"Yes."

Lulwane.

"Oh."

"Yes."

The barking got louder and louder. They could hear the dogs hurling themselves against the fence. "Joseph, it's probably someone for you. I'll make the tea." The water in the pot was beginning to hiss; not long now and it would boil. Reluctantly Joseph got up and picked his way in the dark to the commotion at the gate. George went to fetch the tea leaves. They both liked their tea with milk and sugar but these items were out of stock. Another bat swooped and George, briefly, caught its silhouette against the cloud-struck moon.

"George! George!" called Joseph at the gate, "look here!"

"What is it? I'm coming. Hang on!" The water had just begun to boil, so George added the tea leaves and stirred them with the handle of the relish spoon. He decided to let it boil a little longer, to simmer. He dragged the pot, using the spoon handle, to the edge of the fire; then he went to find Joseph.

"Look," said Joseph pointing to something on the other side of the gate.

"What is it?"

"Hush, dogs, hush! What is it?"

"It must be a child."

George managed to calm the dogs down; then he groped his way to the gate and peered through the diamond mesh. "Let's see. Nothing… nothing. I see nothing, Joseph."

"Not there. On the road."

"Good Lord! Yes, I see it! Looks like a small boy!"

"A small… boy!"

"I'll go and see. Is the gate locked, Joseph?"

"It should be. Wait!" He felt in the back pocket of his trousers and brought out a small key. He released the padlock and unlatched the gate.

"Don't let the dogs out! Please wait for me?" The child was lying face down on the tarmac. The next vehicle to come along would have killed it. "What's the matter, little boy?" said George. The child lay stock-still and said not a word. It was dressed in the rags of poverty, and it stank like abject poverty. "You must get up off the road little boy; otherwise you will be seriously injured." George put his hand on a skinny shoulder. The child didn't flinch. George wondered with alarm if it was still alive. He felt the side of its neck and was relieved to detect a strong pulse.

"It must be street kid," said Joseph. "Let us tell the madam."

"The madam does not like to be disturbed when she is watching videos, and tonight it's a re-run of The Sopranos. But we can't just leave it here to die." George scooped the child into his arms, and was about to return to the gate when he noticed an object on the road. The child had been resting its face on this object. George freed one of his hands, picked it up, and discovered by the light of the moon that it was a little book. He shoved it into a capacious khaki pocket and proceeded to carry the limp creature through the gate – the dogs were curious but calm – and on to his quarters. Joseph locked up and then followed George who had tenderly placed the child on the ground next to the dying fire. It opened its eyes for the first time and looked directly at George; wide brown eyes reflecting the embers and the moonlight. The dogs gathered around it to sniff and to lick. "Let's see if it will drink a little tea. Pity we don't have any milk and sugar. Use my mug, Joseph."

Joseph poured a little of the tea from the pot into George's mug; then he filled his own mug. George blew on the liquid to cool it down. Carefully he placed his hand behind the child's head and lifted it into a drinking position. Its eyes never left George. There was no fear in them, no curiosity; just a kind of world-weariness that you'd expect in the eyes of someone like George. He carried the mug to the child's lips and tilted it gently. A few drops were spilled but most of the liquid went down. Soon the child indicated that it had had enough by closing its eyes and turning its face to the warmth of the fire.

"This is not good," said Joseph gulping down his tea and getting up to go to his shack.

"We'll go to the authorities tomorrow," George replied. "How old do you think he is?"

"As old as the world."

"What do you mean?"

"*Hokoyo*, George, he has been sent by *muroyi*, a witch."

"Nonsense, Joseph, he's just a child, a lost child, sick and starving."

Joseph clicked his tongue and walked away into the night. The dogs followed him to his shack and then returned to the fire. The child seemed to have fallen asleep. George stirred the embers with a stick. He wasn't sure what to do next. Warm some water. Get rid of those filthy rags. Wash the child. Feed it somehow. Mulberries. The tree was laden. He would steal a handful by the light of the moon. He rinsed the pot, filled it with fresh water, and returned it to the middle of the grid. He used the stick to push those embers still glowing directly underneath the pot. While he waited for the water to warm he hummed Brahms' Lullaby, over and over, till the crickets joined in; and then a Scops owl, chirruping.

He went back into his room to find something clean for the little boy to wear. He decided on his navy blue tracksuit top with only a few moth holes. In the days when he refereed school rugby matches he wore that top. He wondered suddenly what had become of his whistle, his boots, his Matabeleland jersey. Packed away in some suitcase somewhere in the house. Now the property of *Inkosikazi* Nyamayakanuna. He took a piece of soap, a towel, and a facecloth from the shower cubicle and returned to the outside fire. The water was warm enough. Gently George lifted the still sleeping child into a semi-standing position. He removed what was left of its shirt and put it into the fire. It was damp so it smoked awhile before the flames took it. He dipped the facecloth in the pot and proceeded to wash the skinny body, starting with the head and moving down to the neck, shoulders, arms, torso. He did not use soap on the child's face lest it got into his eyes (which opened, fixed on George, with the first touch of the wet cloth), but everywhere else was thoroughly washed and rinsed.

He leant the child against his neck and shoulder in order to remove the trousers, which also went into the fire. This time he started at the bottom and worked his way up. First the feet with soles as hard as tortoise-shell, then the skeletal legs – dem bones, dem bones – shins, calves, knees, thighs… soap, dip, rub, rinse… soap, dip, rub, rinse… Finally he came to the tricky part, and discovered that the child was a girl! Nevertheless, George completed the job, as delicately as he knew how, towelled her dry and enveloped her in his tracksuit top. All the while she kept her eyes fixed on George's face. He tucked her up in his bed, climbed in next to her, and soon they were both fast asleep.

10

George woke with a start and discovered the wide-eyed bundle next to him, looking straight into his dream-troubled eyes. "You must be so hungry," he said, "and I have nothing to offer you." Then he remembered the mulberries. He climbed out of bed taking care not to disturb the child, slipped on his tackies, fumbled for his mug, and groped his way toward the mulberry tree on the other side of the madam's house. The dogs always slept outside George's door and now they welcomed him with thumping tails. George had planted that tree from a slip a good fifteen years before, shortly after the previous tree had succumbed to a punishing drought. That year he had lost nearly all his fruit trees. Only a lemon and the guavas had survived. *Psidium guajava.* Another product of ecological imperialism. Joseph had told him that they grew wild, mangoes too, in his home village near Lake Mutarikwa. *Mangifera indica.* Colonising bastards! His pawpaws had gone first, then his oranges and naartjies, then his fig, then his mango, then his avocado pear, then his apricot, then his peach, then, and finally, because he had kept it going with used household water, his catawba grape vine. Apart from the mulberry and another lemon, he replanted his orchard with indigenous fruit trees: *umqokolo* (kei apple), *uzagogwane* (wild cherry), *umkhuna* (wild plum), *umthunduluka,* (sour plum), *umgwadi* (er… monkey-orange) and others. When Beauticious moved in she kept only the mulberry, the lemon, and the largest guava. The rest were designated weeds and had to make way for mealies. After all, this was the start of the mother of all agricultural seasons.

The moon, now directly above the house, gave George sufficient light to select ripe berries. He picked enough to fill his mug and then he returned, the dogs following, to his quarters. He sat the child up and showed her a mulberry. She opened her mouth and he popped it in. He could tell by a slight puckering of her face that she enjoyed the sweet pulp going down. In this way she ate about a dozen before she signalled enough by closing her eyes and turning her face to the bed. Tenderly George let her down and tucked her in. He climbed in next to her and lay on his back with his hands clasped behind his head wondering what he was going to do with this lost little creature. He thought of Perdita in *The Winter's Tale*, of things dying and of things new-born. What did she say about marigolds, his favourite flower?

> *The marigold, that goes to bed wi' th' sun,*
> *And with him rises, weeping; these are flowers*
> *Of middle summer, and I think they are given*
> *To men of middle age…*

Then, without bidding, Wilhelmine swam (or rather, hopped) into his consciousness, and he recalled, with a mingled sense of embarrassment and yearning (is that possible, George?) his second, and final, lesson with her. Prepositions. She thought he was being racist because he took his examples of incorrect usage from black Zimbabweans, examples like 'bored of' instead of 'bored with', and 'picked' instead of 'picked up'. "But Mina," he had countered, "you spend most of your time with black people so it is inevitable that you pick |up| their mistakes."

"Why call them mistakes? Why can't they appropriate the language of oppression, which, since a hundred years, appropriated them?"

"But how does misusing prepositions constitute appropriation?"

"What about blackness in European culture? It is nearly always pejorative."

"I agree with you there, but prepositions are grammatical constructs, they…"

"I suppose you spell 'Africa' with a 'c'! Well, I don't; I spell it the African way, with a 'k'?"

"I don't understand."

"You wouldn't."

"But spelling itself is colonial. It comes with writing…"

"Are you going to tell me that writing did not exist in Africa – with a 'k' – before the white man came along?"

"Certainly not. But I know for a fact that it did not exist in Zimbabwe.

By the way, don't the Germans spell 'Africa' with a 'k'?"

"Er...yes, but..."

"I remember reading all about Rommel's Afrika Corps when I was a boy. Do you know my father fought against Rommel? He was thrashed at Tobruk, and at Alamein he thrashed. Churchill said, 'Before Alamein we never had a victory. After Alamein we never had a defeat'."

At this Wilhelmine looked at George archly and said, "You know you should not talk about the war in front of Germans."

George took this as a peace offering and said, "Well, shall we look at non-racial prepositions?" She nodded assent and pressed her knee (she was wearing bottle-green slacks) against his. George's heart pounded. "Er... talking of Churchill... we were taught at school that it was wrong to put a preposition at the end of a sentence. Churchill demonstrated the absurdity of this rule when he said, 'This is something up with which I will not put'."

"That is not correct?"

"Well, it's clumsy. It should go, 'This is something I will not put up with'. So it's quite acceptable to put a preposition at the end of a sentence."

"But isn't it now an adverb? Doesn't a preposition express a relation to another word or element? In your sentence 'with' is left dangling."

"You've got a point there, Mina. Yes. It isn't always easy to distinguish prepositions and adverbs. For example, in 'he jumped down the slope', 'down' is clearly a preposition: it expresses a relation, as you say, between 'he' and 'slope'. But in 'he jumped down', 'down' functions as an adverb, modifying the verb 'jumped'."

"What about 'he jumped on me'?" (Were her eyelids half-raised or half-lowered?) George's face was instantly transformed into a giant beet-root. His hands began to tremble.

The child had fallen asleep with her mouth open and she began to snore gently. Her first sound! She had gradually moved closer and closer to George and now she was snuggled up against his side. For some time now, indeed some years, George had been aware that his body was har-bouring a guest whose demands, negligible at first, were becoming in-creasingly insistent. His rapidly thinning presence was not just a result of poverty. After all he ate his fill of healthy food every day; and he was all the healthier for not being able to afford even the cheapest alcohol. A slow loss of blood, evident in his narrow, black, irregular stools, made him listless, fatigued. Medical attention was not an option. He was no longer on a Medical Aid scheme, and the government hospitals and clinics had all but collapsed. He would take three-quarters of an aspirin a day until his stock ran out (the other quarter went into the bird bath); then let nature take its course. George had a sentimental attraction to aspirin because its active ingredient, salicylic acid, originated from (or is it 'in', George?) the willow tree, source of the cricket bat, Ophelia's last contact with *terra firma*, symbol of grief and death but also of immortality. It was under a willow tree that Lao Tzu loved to meditate. Was not Moses found floating in a willow basket? It could also be seen as a symbol of miraculous birth. George was pregnant with a foetus lodged in his right colon whose birth would be his death. And now this child, this other guest, gently snoring against his ribs.

Wilhelmine leaned over to George and kissed him gently on the cheek. "*Wir sollen heiter Raum um Raum durchschreiten*, George:

> *An keinem wie an einer Heimat hängen,*
> *Der Weltgeist will nicht fesseln uns und engen,*
> *Er will uns Stuf'um Stufe heben, weiten.*"

Then she gazed at him with speckled eyes, until he dared to look up, and to smile with ill-fitting lips. They trembled like his hands when he said, "'*Weltgeist*' is bullshit, Mina. We might think we feel it but it's an illusion."

"You know some German, George?"

"*Ein Bisschen*, but I read the poem with a dictionary. I spent hours trying to translate it. In the first stanza he says something about a magic force dwelling in all beginnings. I mean, he's nearly as idiotic as Wordsworth! Why does he have to limit this feeling to beginnings? What about middles and endings? Cripes, what has a cosmic spirit got to do with time-trapped concepts like 'beginnings'? In the be-bloody-ginning God created the world! If I want to experience this crap I'll go sit under a willow tree or a Bo-tree, or any tree for that matter. I mean…"

She kissed him full on the mouth. He shuddered. "Let's get back to prepositions, shall we? Is it 'different from' or 'different to' or 'different than'?"

"They're all OK. 'From' is more formal than 'to'. The Americans like to use 'than'."

"Then I can say, 'George is different to most men I know'?"

"Or 'than', or 'from'. Prepositions are idiomatic; there is nothing logical in the way they are used, at least not in English. That's why second language speakers find them so difficult. The Ndebele language works perfectly well without any prepositions."

"Do I blame you 'with' something or 'for' something?"

"'For', but if I'm wrong, don't lay the blame *on* me!"

"That's better, George. You are starting to relax." She tickled him under the chin below which, he painfully knew, swung a dewlap.

The dogs were lapping the dew when George, stretching and yawning, emerged from his room to begin the day's chores. Then he remembered it was Sunday. He gave a sigh of relief and went back to bed.

11

Later that morning the twins came for their lesson on *King Lear*. They brought George a roasted mealie purchased from a road vendor, which he graciously accepted, but put aside for the child (he still couldn't think of it as a girl). The twins also brought news that Hillside Dam was spilling, and George resolved to take a walk there after the lesson.

The boys had done their homework: they understood the terms 'synecdoche' and 'ambivalent', and they had found three examples of paradoxes, all from literature, all indeed from a single text, a play by William Shakespeare called...

"Don't tell me! *Macbeth?*"

"Yes." The twins dropped their eyes.

"And they're all from the first scene of the play? And you got them from your sister?"

"Yes." Searching the ground outside George's *khaya*, for what? Harvester ants? Diamonds?

"Now boys," tut-tutted George, "that is not the way to do research. Can't you think of a single paradox in life? How about fighting for peace? How about having to kill to live? How about needing light to cast a shadow? Remember the mealie? Have you heard the phrase 'true lies', boys? Incidentally, that's called an oxymoron. It's what *King Lear* is about. Remember Edgar's final words?" The boys nodded and took their eyes off the ground.

"'Speak what we feel, not what we ought to say'. Think about it. If you always said what you felt what would happen to you?"

Both boys smiled, then shook their heads. "We would be in big trouble," said Skelter.

"Big, big trouble," his brother affirmed.

"In general we speak our feelings in private, and what we ought to say in public. It's how we cope as social animals. We need ritual, to play roles, to dissemble, in short, to lie. When Lear asks his daughters, in a public, not a private place, 'Which of you shall we say doth love us most', his older daughters, Goneril and Regan go the 'ought to' route, while his youngest, and favourite, daughter, Cordelia, goes the 'feel' route. Which route precipitates the terrible tragedies that follow? Of course you wouldn't know because you haven't even read the play yet. But I'll tell you, boys, it's the 'feel' route. We don't condemn Cordelia for saying what she feels, but for saying what she feels in a public place: a state room in the palace, filled with courtiers.

"At the back of Shakespeare's mind when he wrote *King Lear* was a conflict beginning to tear England apart: the Protestants versus the Catholics; Roundheads against Cavaliers –" (George's thoughts were briefly interrupted by a memory of boarding school where circumcised boys were called 'roundheads', and uncircumcised boys were called 'cavaliers'). "Have you heard of a gentleman called Sir Francis Walsingham?" The boys shook their heads. "Well, sit down and I'll give you a bit of necessary historical background, necessary for the partial understanding – it can only ever be partial – of Shakespeare's greatest play."

The boys made themselves comfortable on the ground while George sat on the step outside his quarters. He had closed the door to his room so that the boys would not discover his secret. "Walsingham created – no boys, don't take notes – the world's first Secret Service, the prototype of MI6, the CIA, the KGB, and our own CIO. Walsingham was rabidly anti-Catholic. He fled England during Mary Tudor's reign of terror. She was known as 'bloody Mary' because of all the Protestants she had killed. While in Paris he witnessed the massacre of French Protestants on St Bartholomew's Eve. When Elizabeth, who, like Shakespeare, was a Protestant in the head (what you ought to say) and a Catholic in the heart (what you feel) – which probably explained her capriciousness (Lear, you know, is capricious)… now where was I? Oh yes, when Elizabeth came to the throne, Walsingham returned to England to serve her and soon became Secretary of State. His secret service was dedicated to the sniffing out of Catholic subversives at home and on the continent. At that time a Spanish invasion of England was imminent. Have you heard of the Armada?"

"Yes, we did it in Form 2 with Mrs Drake."

"Any relation to Sir Francis?"

"She said he was her great, great, great, great granduncle's cousin."

"Very likely," said George sarcastically. "Anyway, once you start paying people to spy on other people you encourage the manufacturing of false information. People start watching each other, listening for sedition, or if there is none, distorting what they hear to make it sound like sedition. 'Get thee glass eyes,' says mad Lear to blind Gloucester, 'and like a scurvy politician, seem to see the things thou dost not'..."

"Please, Sir," asked Helter, "what is sedition?"

"Well, for example, if I replaced a portrait of Robert Gabriel Mugabe for one of Ian Douglas Smith, that would be sedition. Do you understand?"

"I think so."

"It's like going against the authority of the state. Charles Nicholl quotes those words of Lear in his brilliant book about the death of Christopher Marlowe – one of Shakespeare's fellow writers – called *The Reckoning*. I have a copy." George began to get up. "Let me find it and read you a couple of paragraphs." He opened his door just wide enough to squeeze in and was dismayed to see that the child was no longer on his bed. He had brought the mealie with him to give her. He felt a surge of panic as the blood drained from his face. Then he noticed a tortoise shell foot sticking out from under the bed. He almost sobbed with relief. He bent down till he could see all of her, still swaddled in his tracksuit top, and he offered her the mealie. After untangling an arm, she took it gently and immediately began gnawing at it. One thing Beauticious had allowed George to keep, because she was so disgusted by it, was his grandmother's chamber pot, which that incontinent old lady used to keep under *her* bed. George had showed the child how to use it if necessary.

He returned to the boys with the book and a smile on his face. "Are you all right, Sir?" asked Skelter.

"Yes, why?"

"You are smiling."

"Am I? Well, then I am all right."

"But this is your first time for smiling!"

"Really?" He smiled broadly. "Now, listen to this, boys, and ask your-selves if it doesn't sound familiar." He flicked through the pages of Nicholl's book until he found the place he wanted. "Here, listen to this:

'So often |Walsingham's| spies are more than just informers.
They are *agents provocateurs*, or – the more common term then
– 'projectors'. They actively encourage conspiracy. They tout for
sedition. This becomes the classic feature of Walsingham's
tradecraft: at its most cynical, it takes the form of the 'sham plot',
created from the start by Walsingham's projectors, and used as
a means of drawing out genuine Catholics. John Le Carre calls
espionage a 'secret theatre', and I find this applying, time after
time, to Elizabethan espionage. So much was concocted, so
much was unreal…'"

George paused and looked up. "'Secret theatre'", he repeated. "Shake-speare saw the world as a stage. That's an example of synecdoche, where the whole represents the part. It works the other way round. Shakespeare called his theatre (his stage) the Globe (the world). *King Lear* is so much more complex than, for example, *Macbeth*, because it doesn't simplisti-cally link appearances with the |d|evil and reality with Go|o|d. You know, the Biblical idea: God says 'I am that I am'; the devil says 'I am not what I seem to be'. Am I the innocent flower, or am I the serpent under it? The devil does not wear his heart upon his sleeve for daws to peck at. He is an equivocator. Incidentally, his prototype is the God Pan of classical mythol-ogy. He possesses many of Pan's characteristics, but there is one startling difference. Pan is the god of nature (the world); Satan is the god of illu-sion (the stage).

"One of the ways Protestants persecuted Catholics in Shakespeare's time was to destroy their icons, hence the word 'iconoclast'. All those stat-uettes of Jesus, of Mary, of the saints; all those portraits, were smashed. For the Protestants it was idolatrous, illusory, to worship God through an in-termediary. Why not speak directly to the old man? It was this idea of the Protestants, more than anything else in the world, more even than so-cial Darwinism, that freed the individual to such an extent that he began to shake his fist at God for not existing…"

The twins had stopped listening. They wanted to read the play.

"We need ritual; we need to play games; we need to pretend that every mating does not mean a kill. 'O reason not the need', says Lear:

> Our basest beggars
> Are in the poorest thing superfluous.
> Allow not nature more than nature needs,
> Man's life's as cheap as beast's.

"Now where was I? Oh yes, *The Reckoning*. This guy can write! I'd like to read you just a little more." The twins were beginning to look despondent.

> "… no one was quite certain of |the spies'| true allegiances. The better they were at their job, the harder it was to distinguish them from 'genuine' subversives. Even after years of service they remained ambiguous: used but never trusted, spied on even as they were spying.
>
> "We are in the familiar 'wilderness of mirrors' – another phrase from Cold War espionage that is entirely apt for the Elizabethans. A Catholic may be turned, but he is still a Catholic. Perhaps he is playing the double game, so that his role as informer is just another layer of cover. This was a problem for the spymaster, and it is a problem for anyone trying to investigate this business four hundred years later. These people have left behind a paperchase of documents and records, but the things they did and said are always open to diametrically opposed interpretations. Is he a genuine conspirator or an *agent provocateur*. Is he a purveyor of information or disinformation?"

"Excuse me, Sir," asked Helter, "but what is ahshah…prah…?"

"*Agent provocateur*? It's French. It literally means provocative agent. Let me try to explain by example. One of the methods the Fifth Brigade used for sniffing out dissidents was to pretend that they were dissidents. They would dress accordingly and visit some remote village in Thsolotsho, say. Once there they would tell the villagers that they had fled the Mugabe regime, and would beg for food and shelter. The villagers, either sympathetic or afraid, would help them. The next day the *agents provocateurs* would return in their red berets and accuse the villagers of harbouring dissidents."

"What happened to the villagers?"

"They were massacred in their thousands. In one reported incident a pregnant villager had her baby ripped out of her womb and bayoneted in front of her. The soldiers said that her baby was a dissident, and she was harbouring it."

The twins were shocked but shook their heads doubtfully. Helter spoke: "My mother says it was all lies what the Fifth Brigade did, lies made up by the British to besmirch our great nation."

"'There are none so blind as those who will not see'. Ask Gloucester. Ask Lear." An uncomfortable silence ensued so George said, "Let's begin reading, shall we?" They turned with relief to their texts, and George began: "'I thought the King had more affected the Duke of Albany than Cornwall...'"

12

...THE NEED

George read to the boys for about an hour, paraphrasing nearly every line and thoroughly mystifying them with scurrilous assertions that 'nothing' (no thing) was a vagina (0). As if that wasn't enough he linked Lear's 'darker purpose' with Edgar's 'dark and vicious place', insinuating that the King had some sort of guilty incestuous feeling for his daughter. The word 'place', he explained, like 'nothing', was a vagina, and it had that connotation in Cordelia's sarcastic reply to 'the jewels of our father', her sisters:

> But yet, alas, stood I within his grace,
> I would prefer him to a better place.

And later in the play, Regan jealously asks Edmund, 'Have you never found my brother's way / To the forfended place?' She suspects that Edmund has been having sex with Goneril.

George tried to explain, without much conviction, that Shakespeare used female genitalia as a metaphor of Lear's loss of masculine authority, as a king, as a man, and as a father. Doesn't the fool repeatedly call him 'nothing', an 'O without a cipher', a 'shealed peascod'?

"That's a shelled pea-pod, boys."

"Shelled?"

"With all the peas taken out. By the way, if you reverse the word 'peascod' you get 'codpiece'. A codpiece was a sort of leather bag that men wore at the front of their trousers, and it came to symbolise masculinity. Lear isn't the only male character to whom this emasculating imagery is applied. The blinded Gloucester is told to 'smell his way to Dover' (in this play, men are associated with the sense of sight, women with the sense of smell), and who can forget that haunting inversion: 'Edgar I nothing am'? And Albany gets put down in this way by his wife, Goneril. She calls him a 'milk-livered man', and when he says the only thing that restrains him from beating her is her 'woman's shape', she replies mockingly, 'Marry, your manhood! Mew!'"

"Also Lady Macbeth," said Skelter, "she accuses Macbeth of being a coward."

"Yes, and Cleopatra taunts Antony in a similar way."

"Why is it men hate being called cowards?"

"I guess it goes back to the days when men were warriors and hunters. They had to be brave. That was one of the worst effects of colonialism in Africa. It turned warriors into houseboys. How's that for emasculation?"

George smiled at the twins who smiled back. Ultimate called them for lunch, pizza and Coca-Cola from the takeaway at Hillside shopping centre, and they seemed quite relieved that the lesson had come to an end. They wandered indoors with their sister, amazed at how little the synopsis of the play, which their teacher had given them, had to do with it.

George always dressed in his old school clothes on his day off: the powder-blue safari-suit was his favourite, with its loose fit and its capacious pockets. His rapid weight loss had rendered the suit even looser, and the pockets even more capacious. Also on Sundays, he replaced his workaday tackies with his reinforced cardboard shoes (socks, however, from Woolworths), and his tasselled fez with a floppy hat. He was ready to go out walking. He wondered if the mysterious little girl would like to come along. The snowberries were in season, and if they were lucky they might stumble upon some field mushrooms.

She was still under the bed, the pipless mealie cob in her hand. She stared at him with expressionless eyes. "Would you like to go for a walk, child?" asked George in a gentle voice. She did not move until he held out his hand, which she took with hers, and then squirmed out from under the bed. He stood her up and dusted the tracksuit top. He wondered at her age: seven? "Come," he said, "let's go."

Hand in hand they walked to the side gate, Hercules and Ajax anxious to join them but knowing that without the choke chains there was no 'walkies'. George didn't have a key for the padlock and Joseph had been arrested on Friday and was still in custody. The police had stepped up their arrests of poor people since Simba Makoni's announcement that he would stand against Robert Mugabe in the forthcoming presidential elections. Suddenly people were being apprehended for not having lights on their bicycles, or for chatting together in public places. Joseph had been confronted by five policemen, barely out of their teens, on Chinese-made mountain bikes. They demanded to see his bicycle licence. He pointed out the aluminium disc screwed on to the axle of his back wheel. Then they demanded to see his receipt for the purchase of the licence. This, of course, he could not produce. At that point he made the mistake of demanding to see their bicycle licences. He was accused of obstructing the course of the law, severely beaten, and arrested.

George lifted the child over the gate, and then, grimacing with pain, climbed over. This excited the dogs greatly and they had a mock battle while George cried, "Hush dogs, hush". Hand in hand the odd couple walked down Leander Avenue on their way to Hillside Dams. They were stared at curiously by the never ending flow of pedestrian traffic on the potholed roads of suburbia. George marvelled at the number of erstwhile private residences that had been converted into so-called Guest Houses, with names like Traveller's Rest, Inn of Happiness, and My Blue Heaven. Closer to the truth (do you smell a fault, George?) would have been names like the One-Night Stand, the Shag Me Quickly, and the Pump Inn. Even Florence Partridge's house, so recently vacated, was in the process of being converted to a place (Oops, that word!) for men and women who were blocks in the pyramid of Comrade Mugabe's patronage system, and consequently could afford the foreign currency necessary for thirty minutes of bliss with someone much younger and much more beautiful than themselves.

They turned right into Banff Road, still holding hands but exchanging nary a word. They passed an old sign, on the left, from Rhodesian days. The rust had not quite obliterated the words (ironical since the entire Hillside recreational area had become a vast dumping ground for the surrounding dwellings):

NOTICE

NO DUMPING

OFFENDERS WILL BE

PROSECUTED

BY ORDER

TOWN CLERK

There were 'Town Clerk' signs all over Bulawayo, all very bossy. Most of them had been vandalised, but many of them still yielded words of caution. George thought of Shelley's sonnet, 'Ozymandias': 'Look on my works, ye mighty, and despair'.

Past that stately marula under which vendors sometimes display their wares, and which is being seriously damaged by bark gatherers. It is a male. Misguided city dwellers think that its wood yields an aphrodisiac. It is covered in dark red scars where the trunk has been slashed. George thought back to the previous year when he had gathered a basketful of the fruit from a nearby female in order to make jelly, only to be foiled by a countrywide shortage of sugar. The kernels inside the stony nuts were delicious, and so oily that you could set them alight.

The child became quite animated when she saw a pair of creamy butterflies chasing each other from bush to bush. She did a little skip, and George could have sworn that she suppressed a smile: the slight downturn of the mouth, the slight creasing of the skin on the sides of the eyes. A party of red-billed hoopoes, one with a worn tail, dipped across the road cackling like the witches in an amateur production of *Macbeth*. It was a beautiful late summer's day. The atmosphere was squeaky clean after weeks of cyclonic rainfall. The antiseptic blue sky was dotted about with cotton wool clouds. George had heard the little girl snore, and now he heard her sigh – with delight.

Not only was the upper dam spilling but the lower dam was full. The dense bush glowed orange (Isn't that your favourite colour, George?) with tithonia, a Mexican colonial. George picked |no preposition required| one of the hollow-stemmed flowers and offered it to his companion. She took it, scrutinised it, and handed it back to George. "There's a story behind that flower," he said, not sure if she understood a word of English. "Aurora, the goddess of the dawn fell in love with a beautiful young man called Tithonus. She made him immortal but she forgot to give him eternal youth. Consequently he grew old and withered while she remained ever young. His immortality became a torment to him and he begged to be allowed to die. Aurora could not do this but out of pity, she transformed him into a grasshopper. "You see, this flower is the colour of the dawn, Aurora's immortal beauty reflected in the face of Tithonus, no longer the shrivelled old man who cannot die, but a transient bloom."

A slow clapping startled him, and there on a stone bench partly hidden by a lichen-spattered boulder, flanked by two young men, sat Wilhelmine. George first saw a triptych for an altar: The Madonna with two of the darker complexioned wise men bearing gifts. Next he saw the Mina he had metamorphosed into literature, his *belle dame sans merci*, his freckled green thought, his Desdemona about to be smothered by the Moor, his Portia giving the Prince of Morocco a gentle riddance. Finally he saw Mina, the German NGO: pretty, young, intelligent, and resembling a grasshopper. The man on her left was slender, androgynous with his dreadlocks and his sling bag. He gave George and the child a warm smile. The man on her right, by contrast, was overly masculine. He was short and stocky and he had shaved his head bald. He looked George's safari suit up and down. "You know," he said, and George immediately recognised his voice, "that outfit of yours is a collector's item. How much do you want for it?"

"It's not for sale. Aren't you…"

"I am a collector of Rhodesiana. The stuff sells like hot cakes overseas. Last week I sold a copper portrait of Ian Smith for thirty five pounds sterling. I'll give you a hundred |meaning a hundred million| for that safari suit."

It sounded like a lot of money for someone on a domestic worker's salary, and George had already worried about getting the little girl some clothes, so he agreed to the transaction.

"A bargain," laughed Wilhelmine. "Who is the little boy?"

"It's a girl," said George. "We're friends."

"How sweet!" Dreadlocks had begun to fondle the back of her neck, and she responded by half shutting her eyes, a gesture which made George gasp. "You're just a jealous old man, George."

"I…"

"Hey, I know you," interrupted glans-head, "you are the honkie who called me 'kaffirman'. Can you beat that!" he said turning to Wilhelmine, "he called me a 'kaffirman' to my face!"

"I'm not surprised," said Wilhelmine, "these Rhodies are the most racist people on earth; or is it in earth, Mr George?" She rested her hand on dreadlock's thigh and left it there. George turned to walk away. He dropped the flower but the little girl picked it up and offered it to him. "What about your hot pants, old man?" said Wilhelmine.

Glans-head pulled a wad of money from his back pocket and counted out ten ten-million dollar notes. "Here. Now get out of your clothes!"

"You mean…"

"You heard the man, George. Off!"

"'Off, off, you lendings! Come, unbutton here.'" While George fumbled with his buttons, glans-head came over, took the flower out of his hand and stuck it behind George's ear. Luckily George wore underpants on Sundays, so he wouldn't have to go stark naked. Off came the jacket, down went the trousers. He had to sit on a rock in order to work them over his shoes. The little girl sat with him. "Do you know, Mina, that your friend is a plain-clothed policeman?"

"CIO, George. Both my friends are CIO."

He finally got his trousers off, inside out, and handed them to glans-head. "And you know that they torture people?"

"Who are you to speak of torture, George? You tortured an entire race of people."

"I am a synecdoche."

"A what?"

"Synecdoche." He stood up with some effort, looking ridiculous in underpants, shoes and socks. His skeleton could be studied under the palimpsest of his withered flesh. "The part that represents the whole."

"No hole for your part," grinned dreadlocks who, up to that point, had seemed sympathetic to George's plight. His friends laughed at the joke, and even George, who couldn't resist a pun, was obliged to smile.

George tucked the money behind the elastic of his underpants, and held his hand out to the child. "Come, dear," he said, "Let's go and look for snowberries." He glanced back once and caught his final, indelible image of Wilhelmine: she was going down on her knees.

They soon found a bush, on their way to the spilling upper dam. It was loaded with fruit. George broke off a branch and handed it to the child who seemed to recognise it. She let go of his hand in order to give full attention to the waxy white berries.

A number of people had gathered at the point where the dam was spilling, some to paddle, some to catch tadpoles, and some to watch. A few fisherman, domestic workers like George on their day off, were perched close to the deeper water's edge throwing in their lines and, for hours, catching nothing. George's appearance caused some consternation. People didn't know whether to be shocked or amused, so they settled for both. He greeted them politely and showed the little girl how to paddle in the shallow but fast-running water. She squealed (her third sound) but seemed to love the force of the current as it swirled round her ankles. She would have stayed there if George, growing increasingly embarrassed by the stares and the giggles and the clicking of tongues, hadn't called her out.

They were going to return along the dam wall but there were too many people about so they took another route through thick bush where they found themselves alone. "Look, mushrooms!" cried George as they came across an ant-hill carpeted in white termitomyces. "Tonight, little girl, we feast!" They picked as many mushrooms as they could carry. They walked a little further and found themselves in an open, sandy location and there, growing in profusion, was wild lettuce. They put down their mushrooms and picked about twenty of the sharply toothed leaves, which George secured, like the money, behind the elastic of his underpants. They gathered their mushrooms and made their way home, George taking care to avoid the lichen-splattered boulder where he located the image of a kneeling woman whom he loved to distraction.

13

George was preparing potato fritters when Ultimate came into the kitchen with her copy of *Macbeth*. George smiled. The daughter of Beauticious was still at an age when everything interested her. She had not yet been overwhelmed by the aspirations of the new Zimbabwe, and might even find her own way. "You said you would talk to me about metre, George."

"I did indeed, Miss Ultimate, I did indeed. Can you fetch a piece of paper and a pencil?" Ultimate went out again and George continued to grate the raw potatoes, all the way from Peru (all right, George, you've made your point), into a large mixing bowl. He added a cupful of chopped spring onions, salt and pepper. Finally he poured in the batter and mixed the ingredients with a wooden spoon. He had consciously to avoid the redundant adverb, 'together', as in 'mix together', which may be found in any number of tautological cookery books. The sunflower oil in the frying pan was just beginning to sizzle. George was in a relaxed mood for two reasons: Beauticious was away, with the minister, at a conference in Sun City, South Africa. Representatives from all the neighbouring countries, at the South African taxpayers' expense, were gathering in five-star splendour to discuss which aspect of racist-colonialist-imperialism was responsible for the recent power outages. Beauticious had settled for Blair's kith and kin but the minister thought they should go further back in time, and he laid the blame squarely on the shoulders of the late Frederick Courteney Selous. The other reason for George's relaxed mood was the book he discovered in the pocket of his khaki shorts while he was getting dressed for work.

Ultimate returned with paper and pencil, and waited impatiently for George to rinse and dry his hands. "All right, Miss Ultimate," he said taking the paper and pencil, "can you remember the third paradox in that opening scene?"

"Yes, it's 'Fair is foul and foul is fair'."

"Good." George wrote the words on the paper, spacing them apart, and scanning them:

$$\text{F\={a}ir \v{i}s / f\={o}ul, \v{a}nd / f\={o}ul \v{i}s / f\={a}ir}$$

"See? That's how you scan a line of poetry. The trochee is disyllabic, a two syllable foot separated by an oblique line called a virgule. Say it!"

"Virgule."

"Good. Now the symbol that indicates a stressed syllable is called a macron. Say it!

"Macron."

"Good. The symbol that indicates an unstressed syllable is called a breve. Say it!"

"Breve."

"Well done! If you count the feet in the line you will find that there are three and a half; the last syllable is lacking. We call that catalectic. Say it!"

"Catalectic,"

"That's to avoid a weak, or feminine (oops), ending as, for example in these lines from one of Feste's songs:

> Trip no further, pretty sweeting:
>
> Journey's end in lovers meeting.

"These lines have their full number of syllables (eight in all) so they are called acatalectic. A line with an extra syllable is called hypercatalectic, while a line which is more than one syllable short is called brachycatalectic…"

"Don't ask me to say those!"

George smiled. He had begun frying the fritters and they gave off a delicious smell. When each batch was ready he drained them on a paper lined tray. They were distracting his pupil so he offered her one to test for quality. "Don't burn yourself now! Blow on it." She crunched away happily. "So the witches speak in trochaic tetrameter catalectic."

"What about:

> Double, double toil and trouble.
>
> Fire burn, and cauldron bubble?"

"Clever girl! All the syllables are there so it's acatalectic. The important point is that the witches who represent chaos, speak in trochees (stressed, unstressed), while the humans speak in blank verse, which is predominantly iambic (unstressed, stressed). At the thematic level of prosody you could say that a perfect iambic pentameter line, for example: 'and all our yesterdays have lighted fools…' represents order, and any alteration thereof represents degrees of disorder culminating in the completely inverted metre of the witches."

"Can you give me an example of a line which is somewhere in between?" asked Ultimate.

"Well, take the next line of Macbeth's lament: 'the way to dusty death. Out, out, brief candle!' The first six syllables are perfectly iambic. And then you get four stressed syllables in a row followed by an unstressed syllable. Incidentally, that last syllable is extra…"

"Hype…"

"Hypercatalectic. It's especially weak in contrast to the four stressed syllables that precede it. Consequently it has a guttering effect – a dying light."

"How would you scan the four stressed syllables?"

There are no four-syllable feet in English prosody, so you'd have to split them."

"How?"

"Well, prosody is not an exact science, but I would suggest grouping 'out, out, brief' as a rare foot called molossus, and then 'candle' can be a trochee."

"How is this going to help me with the exams?"

"Not much, I'm afraid. What would you like with your potato fritters? An omelette?"

"Mushroom?"

"I think we can arrange that."

"Yummy! Thank you, George."

"You're welcome, Miss Ultimate." George still had a good supply of mushrooms from Hillside Dams. Those he and the child had not eaten, he had sun-dried and hung on a washing line, taking care that they didn't touch each other. As soon as the fritters were done he would fetch the mushrooms and soak them in water for a while before cooking them. With Beauticious away he would filch a fritter and a portion of the omelette for his companion, who was growing healthier by the day. Her complexion had begun to shine, and her hair looked less rusty. Her new used clothes, which George had purchased from a roadside vendor, were most becoming, George thought: a red long-sleeved shirt and a pair of sturdy blue jeans. "Now, what are the very first words Macbeth speaks?"

"I remember, George; it's… um… 'So foul and fair a day I have not seen.' It's the witches' words. It shows that he's already in their power."

"Yes, and there's an interesting difference. Let us scan the line. You try. First write it down making a space between each word." Ultimate wrote the line below George's. Now, separate the feet with virgules."

"Oblique lines?"

"Yes. Go on… Good. Count the feet."

"One, two, three, four, five?"

Correct. That's called a pentameter. Now add the macrons and the breves above the syllables. Look at my example… No, it's the other way round. Say the line aloud exaggerating the rhythm."

"So FAIR and FOUL a DAY I have not SEEN."

"Nearly, but you have to assert the metre a little. The first three feet lead you to expect an emphasis, not on 'I' (which generally is emphasised), but on 'have'. Try again."

"So FAIR and FOUL a DAY i HAVE not SEEN."

"That's it! By George, you've got it!"

"'By George'?"

"It's a line from a musical called *My Fair Lady*."

"Isn't that racist, George?"

"What?"

"I mean, *fair* lady."

"I'd say it's more sexist than racist. Perhaps it's a combination, as when Macbeth calls the witches 'secret black and midnight hags'. Since it's a key word in your play why don't you look it up in my… er… your Concise Oxford. Meanwhile" (the fritters were done) "I'll go find some mushrooms for the omelette."

Ultimate dashed off to get the dictionary while George, struggling with a sharp pain in his stomach, dragged himself outside.

She was back long before him, impatiently waiting to read him the entry for 'fair'. "Wow! It's a lot of stuff, George."

He filled a pot with water to soak the mushrooms. "Well, go on... let's hear it."

"OK. *Fair*. One: 'just, unbiased, equitable; in accordance with the rules'..."

"Is that racist?"

"No. Two: 'blond; light or pale in colour or complexion'..."

"Is that?"

"What?"

"Racist."

"It could be; depends on the context, I guess."

"Go on."

"Three: 'of (only) moderate quality or amount; average.'"

"Is that?"

"Could be. But there's a variation of Three: 'considerable, satisfactory (a *fair* chance of success)'. Then Four: '(of weather) fine and dry; (of the wind) favourable'. Five: 'clean, clear, unblemished (*fair* copy)' Six: 'beautiful, attractive'... couldn't that be racist, George? Doesn't it imply that dark is ugly and unattractive?"

"Foul?"

"Yes, foul – like in *Macbeth*."

"It could. It's the way we think, in opposites, binary, like computers. That's how sentences are structured: subject/object... no synapse..."

"We did that in biology. It passes impulses between two nerve cells."

He transferred the mushrooms to a colander. "Biological epiphany."

"I beg yours?"

"Nothing, dear; go on with 'fair'."

"OK, where was I?"

"You had just completed Six."

"Right. Here we are. Seven: 'archaic kind, gentle.' Eight has two parts: 'specious...' what does that mean, George?"

"It's like an argument that seems to be right but is actually wrong." He pressed the mushrooms dry with a paper napkin.

"Then it goes on: '(fair speeches)' and then: 'complimentary (fair words)'. That's Eight; now Nine... er... what? 'Austral & NZ'!"

"That's Australia and New Zealand. What does it go on to say?"

"'Complete unquestionable...'"

"*Fair* dinkum."

"And then it just goes on and on... I've had enough!" The dictionary thudded shut.

"'Words, words, words – I'm so sick of words'"

"Me too, George; can I have another fritter? She filched one before he could reply, and skipped out of the kitchen.

"You can and you may, but don't tell your brothers; which reminds me: I have to fetch them from rugby practice. What's the time?" He dried his hands on a dishcloth and went to peer at the clock on top of the fridge. Before He could focus on the hands and the numbers an insistent hooting began at the gate. "Who comes round on a Friday afternoon when the madam is away?"

BEEP BEEP BEEEEP, BEEP BEEP BEEEEP (anapaestic dimeter).

"Coming! Crikey, I'm coming!"

14

"Mr George?"

"Yes? Oh, no!" George had taken care to lock the dogs in the garage. They were barking furiously. He wished now that he'd left them in the yard.

"Mr George George?"

"Yes. George J. George."

"Of 43…"

"Leander Avenue, Hillside. Yes."

"Mr George, last Sunday you were observed walking naked in a public place."

"I wasn't naked, I…"

"I'm arresting you for public indecency."

"All right officer, I'll come, but please would you allow me to organise some food for a child who is staying with me?"

"If you make it quick."

"I'll be quick." He hobbled back to the kitchen, put all the fritters on a plate, and took them to his *khaya*. The child was sitting on the doorstep drawing something in the sand with a stick. She looked at him with not quite expressionless eyes. There was a glint of expectation. George offered her the fritters, told her he had to go away for a while, urged her to keep out of sight, he would be back as soon as possible. Did she understand a word? The he returned to the kitchen where he found Ultimate's pen and paper. He wrote: I HAVE BEEN ARRESTED. SORRY. BACK SOON. DOGS ARE IN THE GARAGE. He placed the note on the dining room table and hobbled back to the policeman. There were two others in the blue Santana whose engine was still running. A back door opened for him to climb in. He was immediately placed in handcuffs.

The woman officer looked him up and down and said, "Why are you dressed like that?"

"I…"

"Isn't it you look like a kaffir?" They all burst out laughing while the driver changed gear and drove off.

At the charge office George caused some consternation because he had no shoes to remove. So they took his fez and pushed him into the same overcrowded cell as last time. Before he could get his bearings, a hoarse voice called out "*Uthini*, George?"

It was Joseph. "Joseph!" cried George, "good to see you," and they shook hands. "Didn't you get the bail money I sent?"

"Yes, but they wouldn't grant me because they say I resisted arrest. Why are you here?"

"Public indecency."

"What?"

"I was walking around the dams in my underpants."

Just then the cell door opened and a guard came in with a tattered paperback in his hands. "Mr George!" he barked. George held up his hand like a school pupil. "The Chief Inspector says you must read the first two chapters of this book before he sees you for questioning." He held the book out and George took it: *A Grain of Wheat* by the Kenyan writer, Ngugi wa Thiong'o. He knew it well. It had been an A-level set work some years before.

"Bastard wants another free lesson," he muttered.

"What did you say?" from the guard.

"Nothing… er… a mosquito bit me." The guard shook his head in contempt and exited the cell.

The prisoners, this time round, seemed quite lively. The cell was abuzz with talk of the forthcoming 'harmonised' presidential and parliamentary elections. News of Simba Makoni's late entry into the fray had given the vast underclass of Zimbabwe new hope. Someone had smuggled in an article from the English newspaper, *The Independent*, in which Makoni was quoted to have said, "I share the agony and anguish of all citizens that we all have endured for nearly ten years now. I also share the view that these hardships are a result of failure of national leadership."

George thought he was the only white in the cell until his tired eyes fell on… he couldn't believe it… his old headmaster. He was sitting down in a corner of the cell with his elbows on his knees and his hands on his ears. He looked quite comical in bare feet and a worsted grey suit. George shuffled over to Mr Sylvester Crackling MA, PCE, and tapped him on the shoulder. "Headmaster," he said, "how are you otherwise?"

The Head creaked out of his position of despondency and blinked at the quondam English teacher. "Not surprised to see you here, George. What was it, drunken driving?"

"No, Sir, public indecency. And you?"

"That figures. I attempted to expel the Chief Inspector's son for selling US dollars in the urinals, during break time."

"Do you have a lawyer?"

"I did have, but he diasporised a few days ago. Bastard."

"How long have you been inside?"

"An eternity."

"Is anybody looking after you?"

"The staff sent me a card with butterflies edged in glitter and a note saying 'come back soon'."

"What about food?"

"Miss Poops is attending to that. She brings me a Tupperware of curried vegetables every evening, and a bottle of soda water when available."

"Mr George!" called a guard from the cell door, "do not keep the Chief Inspector waiting!"

"Coming," said George. "Excuse me, Headmaster, a have a lesson to teach."

Mr Sylvester Crackling MA, PCE gave George a baleful look, muttered "Twerp," and returned his face to his hands.

The sound of Brenda Fassie in full cry greeted George's ears before his face-to-face greeting with the Chief Inspector. "Ah, Mr George," cried that dignitary, pumping his hand in a manner unAfrican, "how good to see you again. By the way, I received a distinction for my *Hamlet* essay."

"Congratulations," said George without enthusiasm.

"Don't be such a sour puss, Mr George! What is the matter with you white people? You have so much going for you. Don't you realise that as the owner of a house and a motor car, you are among the top two percent of the world's wealthy? I won't even go into the fact that you stole that property from our people."

"Sorry, I'll try to cheer up. It's just that I'm very worried…"

"Nothing to worry about, Georgy boy. As soon as you've given me some assistance with this damn assignment I'll let you go. You won't even have to sign an admission of guilt form. Now sit down and I'll bring you a glass of Fanta orange. There's no Coke in the shops." He stopped the music, went over to his little fridge and pulled out an almost empty family size bottle of Fanta. "Not much left, I'm afraid, but times are hard." He poured it all into a glass and handed it to the prisoner. George thanked him, sipped it, and grimaced at its flatness. "I see you've got that copy of *A Grain of Wheat*; did you manage to read the first two chapters?"

"It wasn't necessary. I know the book. I taught it some years ago."

"That's good news, Georgy. You see I have this assignment, already overdue – but I have managed to get an extension – which requires me to analyse in detail the book's beginning and to relate it to the concerns of the book as a whole. I haven't managed to read it yet – my farms are taking up so much of my time – first too much rain then too little – what with the mother of all agricultural seasons pending, that I sometimes don't know whether I'm Arthur or Martha, Mr George, Arthur or Martha…"

"Shall we begin?"

"Of course. And this time I'll use a Dictaphone – police property so I'm not really supposed to use it for private purposes, but what the hell, hey Georgy, what the hell!" While he spoke he set the Dictaphone up so that George could speak into it. "Luckily we've got power tonight."

George turned to the first page of the paperback and scanned it. "The novel begins…"

"Hang on. It's not connected. OK, go ahead."

"The novel begins with a simple sentence: 'Mugo felt nervous.' Who is Mugo?…"

"Wait, Mr George. Could you give me a synopsis of the chapter? As I said, I haven't had a chance to read it yet."

George sighed. He gave a synopsis and then said, "Now do you want me to analyse the chapter for you?"

"In relation to the novel as a whole, please, Mr George. How's your Fanta?"

"Fine, thank you." George hadn't touched it after the first sip. "Right, well… we need to ask why Mugo is nervous. Straight away, you see, the reader is engaged. Mugo is experiencing a nightmare filled with images of torture…" George had his eyes on the text… "the drop of water suspended above his face, about to fall; he is 'chained' to his bed; and these images will carry over to his wakened state, when the water will 'pierce' his eyes. (Water develops into one of the many motifs of this novel). People who have nightmares often suffer from anxiety or guilt in their waking lives. Does Mugo have secrets to hide? Are we to assume that, since he is the first character we meet, he will have an important role to play in the novel? We are not yet given a physical description of Mugo (we must read on for that!), but we learn that he is very poor. His blanket is 'hard and worn out'; his breakfast is meagre. It seems that he is a peasant, and we are reminded of Ngugi's short preface where he aligns his sympathies with the peasants of Kenya." George turned back to the preface and read part of it out: "'the peasants who fought the British yet now see all that they fought for being put to one side.'

"At the end of the opening paragraph we are given some extra information, which adds to our awakening curiosity. Mugo has been in detention. Perhaps this is why he is having nightmares. We are also introduced, briefly, to an interesting narrative technique. The novel begins in the third person, where the author remains outside the story, referring to the fictional character, Mugo, as 'he', 'his', 'him'. And it is written in the past tense: 'he was lying on his back'. But towards the end of the paragraph we read: 'How time drags, everything repeats itself…' We shift briefly into the present tense, and we also shift into Mugo's mind, which brings us closer to him. This is called direct interior monologue. Put it in the past tense: 'How time dragged, everything repeated itself', and you have indirect interior monologue. Ngugi takes us into Mugo's mind more than any of the other characters, which also suggests his importance in the novel…"

George became conscious of a gentle snoring. He looked up from the text and saw that the Chief Inspector's head was nodding. He's also bald, George realised for the first time. Why do the cops all want to look like Yul Brynner? (Don't you mean Michael Jordan, George?) Well, the Dictaphone was still on, so he might as well continue. He wouldn't be let out until the lesson, lecture more likely, was over.

He returned his eyes to the text: "One of Ngugi's concerns in this novel is to explore the double bind of African women who suffered not only at the hands of the colonial regime but within their own culture where they were sometimes brutally treated by their menfolk. So, in this first chapter and beyond, women are generally presented in heroic terms... er... quote: 'Mugo found that some women had risen before him, that some were already returning from the river, their frail backs arched double with water-barrels, in time to prepare tea or porridge for their husbands or children.' On his way to and from his *shamba* Mugo reluctantly greets other characters who will feature in this novel, and Ngugi introduces an extremely effective narrative technique called dialogue... er..."

On and on George droned, picking at the text like a monkey picking at fleas. The Chief Inspector had begun to snore loudly, like one of his numerous redistributed tractors. He was no longer nodding; his head was thrown back, his mouth was wide open, and the skin on his neck was bunched like a coiled mamba.

George continued: "Next we meet Githua, the rather unpleasant village clown. He has lost a leg and he claims, quote... hang on, where is it... quote: 'the white man did this to me with bullets'. He is lying, as we discover later in the novel. According to General R, Githua lost his leg in a traffic accident. When Mumbi wonders why people like Githua have to make up such stories, General R says something which touches on another important theme of the novel, quote: 'He invents a meaning for his life, you see. Don't we all do that?' and to die fighting for freedom sounds more heroic than to die by accident. People's life stories are continually being re-created; history is continually being re-written; fact metamorphoses into fiction, fiction into fact. As the critic Raymond Williams says: 'Tradition is not the past, but an interpretation of the past: a selection and valuation of ancestors, rather than a neutral record.'

"Before he leaves Mugo alone Githua says something, which seems to contradict his buoyant mood, and which resonates throughout the novel, quote: 'The Emergency destroyed us.' The Mau Mau uprising against the British was largely a peasant uprising, mainly from Ngugi's tribe, the

Gikuyu. After a protracted armed struggle in the early fifties they forced the British to capitulate, but not before thousands of them had perished in the so-called 'detention camps', which the British set up after they declared a State of Emergency.

"For Mugo the village streets are dusty, and when he walks he raises dust. At his *shamba*, quote: 'dust flew into the sky, enveloped him'. Where, he wonders, was the, quote: 'fascination he used to find in the soil before the Emergency'. Soil is an important motif: it symbolises the African people who have a spiritual connection to the soil, which was never understood or appreciated by the European colonisers. Because Mugo has betrayed his people, the soil for him turns to dust, and it torments him. The motif, so prevalent in the plays of Shakespeare, to whom Ngugi frequently alludes, is a powerful narrative device in this novel. The train is a motif of colonialism; the dog is a motif of the white settlers; the forest is a motif of the freedom fighters, and so on.

"The enigmatic old woman is first referred to in this chapter, quote: 'Nobody knew her age: she had always been there, a familiar part of the old and the new village.' She is the only character in the novel, as far as I can remember, who is not given a name, which frees her, somehow, from the limitations of time and space. It is interesting that she is isolated, neglected, within her own community. She seems to symbolise a time before Africa became tainted by colonialism, bearing in mind that colonialism in Africa goes back to the sixteenth century. That period takes on a utopian aura. The old woman's intense bond with her mute (pre-articulate?) and virile son, Gitogo, reinforces this; and his violent, unnecessary death by a callous white man seems to symbolise the destruction of primordial innocence. This old woman will be a powerful force in Mugo's destiny.

"The story of Gitogo's death is retrospective. This is Ngugi's dominant narrative technique. The novel's present, the few days before Uhuru in, I think, December 1963, takes up comparatively little space in the text. We continually go back in time through the eyes of the different protagonists, which gives us insight into their psychological complexities, and how their domestic needs conflicted with their political commitment. Much of the novel's dramatic irony is a result of the retrospective, for instance the reader knows that Mugo betrayed Kihika long before the fictional characters get to know it.

"Another narrative technique popular with Ngugi is what T.S. Eliot called the objective correlative , where the objective world, the world out there, correlates sympathetically with the subjective world, the world within the consciousness of the character or characters. For example... where did I see it... oh yes... for example, Mugo's negative feelings are metaphorically echoed by the world around him, quote: 'In the *shamba* he felt hollow. There were no crops on the land and what with the dried up weeds... the country appeared sick and dull.'"

Thus George, the pedantic English teacher, in full throttle -- on and on *ad nauseam*. How many children, in his time, had he put to sleep? After the analysis finally ended, a minute of George's silence woke his interrogator who pretended he had been awake all the time. He switched off the Dictaphone. "That's enough synopsis, George, let's get on with the analysis. How's your Fanta? What on earth were you doing walking around naked at the Hillside Dams? One of my officers spotted you there. 'Thou art the thing itself.'"

"'Unaccommodated man'."

"'Poor, bare, forked animal'. God I wish we didn't have to study these local authors. Come on, Georgy boy, let's do this!" He switched on the Dictaphone.

15

"We stand back from the narrative and reflect on the Party: how it was born, how it grew, from the leadership of Waiaki at the turn of the twentieth century, through Harry Thuku in the 1920s, to Jomo Kenyatta in the 1950s, who took the party to Independence in 1963 We get a potted account of the arrival of the white man: first the missionaries, then the soldiers, then the settlers; how at first the Africans could not take them seriously because they looked ridiculous with the, quote: 'skin so scalded that the black outside had peeled off'; but before long it was the whites who were laughing as, by force and fraud, they entrenched themselves in the land of the Agikuyu. The fact that these white people were ruled over by a woman, Queen Victoria, did not surprise the black people of Kenya since they too, in the remote past, had female rulers like the legendary Wangu Makeri…"

… Ah, Wangu Makeri. She danced naked in front of the menfolk, driving them crazy with desire. Wilhelmine had done it to George, in a scantily furnished lounge somewhere in Kumalo suburb; a house, once a home, that had indulgently nurtured two generations of Rhodesians, all of them now gone, gone back to the Diaspora, or to the Jewish cemetery in Athlone.

He recalled the unpolished parquet floor covered in tiny paper stars, the altar candle burning without a flicker in the stillness of that night, until a huge emperor moth with comb-like antennae and staring eyespots, guttered it. He had been seriously drunk, on bottle after bottle of Private Cellar *cordon rouge*, a medium bodied red wine with, according to the label, fine berry flavours and a rich plum jam aroma. Gentle tannin provide|d| fullness and a lingering ripe fruit finish. Jane Birkin was gasping *J'taime* while outside a million cicadas were shrieking. He recalled the pain in his knees as he crawled towards that swaying body, those penthouse lids half closing eyes, which mocked him, he later realised, to the core of his being. His liver-spotted hands took brief possession of those

96

gyrating hips, and he buried his face in her crotch -- nothing i' the middle -- and found with his tongue her clitoris. It grew enough for him to take it in his chipped teeth and nibble it. Wilhelmine was sighing with pleasure, but nothing to match Jane's theatrical breathing, or the excited Christmas beetles. He drew his hands in until his thumbs were placed on the lips, the parings, which he parted; then he lifted his head away so he could look. It was about a centimetre long and as blue as a shorting cable.

"Let's do it, George," purred Wilhelmine. "We'll try the Twenty-Third Manner, *El khouariki*. Come." She cupped her hands on either side of his cheeks and guided him to a standing position; then she took one of his elbows and led him to a room, which was empty except for a mattress on the floor. With slow deliberation she unbuttoned his safari suit jacket, pushed it over his shoulders, pulled it down his arms, and dropped it onto the floor. She unclasped and unzipped his safari suit trousers, and let gravity take them down. Then she lay on the mattress, opened her legs and waited. George hesitated because he realised that, unspeakable desire notwithstanding, he didn't have an erection. He hated his body for betraying him, and the more he hated it the more it refused to co-operate.

"I'm sorry, Mina," he muttered, "I'm too drunk." (Are you sure that's the reason, George?)

"You white men," said Wilhelmine with contempt, "You are all castrated. 'Know, O my brother (to whom God be merciful), that a man who is misshapen, of coarse appearance, and whose member is short, thin and flabby, is contemptible in the eyes of women.'"

George began to dress himself, trousers first. "You are familiar with *The Perfumed Garden?*"

"Familiar! It is my Bible!"

"But it was written by a man who was a sexist by all accounts." He cursed his zip, which had stuck half way.

"Shaykh Nefzawi knew how to give a woman pleasure." She had closed her grasshopper legs and turned on to her side.

George was almost amused by her bumlessness, though her small breasts were shapely. "He accuses women in general of treachery. He says their tricks will deceive Satan himself."

"You are such a loser, George. Now take your belongings and go. It isn't too late for inviting some friends around. *Raus, du Wurm!*"…

… The Chief Inspector impatiently switched off the Dictaphone. "What is the matter with you, George? Why have you gone silent?"

George snapped out of his reverie. "Sorry… er… where was I?"

The Chief Inspector fiddled with the Dictaphone until he found George's last words: 'Wangu Makeri'

"Right," said George, "Wangu Makeri."

"Now go on, please."

George consulted his text. "Er… the second half of the chapter returns to the narrative, a retrospective account of a political rally held by the freedom fighter, Kihika (a fictional character). We learn that Mugo, for various reasons, hates Kihika. We are introduced to Kihika's beautiful sister, Mumbi, who plays a central role in the novel. We are given an account of the attack by Kihika and his followers on the Mahee police station, Kihika's, quote: 'greatest triumph'. Somebody betrays Kihika and he is captured, tortured, and put to death: a sacrifice from which the party gains strength, and grows.

"That's the synopsis."

"OK, now let's have the analysis, please."

"Well, we notice how Ngugi begins to blur the distinction between fact and fiction by introducing phrases like, here on page eleven, 'so the people say', and on page twelve, 'so it is said', And just as we saw two Mugos emerging, earlier, we now see two Kihikas emerging: the 'real' Kihika and the mythologised Kihika. This is one of the great themes of *A Grain of Wheat*, the theme that obsessed Shakespeare…"

"Appearence versus reality."

"Indeed."

"'The truest poetry is most feigning'."

"Why, yes! Ngugi connects this theme to that of betrayal, which is dramatically expressed in the Swahili proverb: *Kikulacho kiko nguoni mwako* (those who are closest to you are the ones who betray you). Jesus, Ghandi, Malcolm X, were all betrayed by those closest to them. It's another poignant irony of this novel that Kihika sees role models in Jesus and Ghandi. Incidentally, the exploitation of this proverb, or aphorism, as well as, in later chapters, the use of songs and allegorical tales is yet another narrative technique of the novel. These are aspects of the oral tradition, or orature, which enriched African culture before the white man brought the written word…"

"Spare me the humbug, Georgy!"

"I… er. Do you want to hear what the German author, Hans Magnus Enzensberger says about this?"

"Go on."

George went on, and on, and on… about illiteracy, the novel as a product of European culture, and the author's consequent ironic use of it; Ngugi's symbolic presentation of the train, which brings both good and bad to Africa, the bad being somehow good and the good being somehow bad; Ngugi's biblical and Shakesperean allusions; his support for that most precious quality of African culture, *Harambee*; the dialectic of history and propaganda; the dialectic of domestic and political life – George loved the word 'dialectic' because it underscored man's binary nature – the dialectic of loyalty and betrayal… on and on… He dissected the most significant characters like Kihika, Mumbi, Gikonyo, Karanja, John Thompson, and, of course, Mugo. He used words like 'deracination' and 'Messianic' and 'emasculating'.

"Do you get my point?"

"I get your point, Georgy."

"Brief references to Mumbi and Gikonyo in this chapter are not insignificant. Not only is Mumbi very beautiful, she is compared by some to the legendary ruler…er… Wangu Makiri. Her name connects her to another, this time mythological, ruler, Moombi: the first Gikuyu woman, mother of the nation, a moulder, potter, creator. Gikonyo is twice called a carpenter, a trade which links him to Joseph, the father of Jesus…"

"Did you know that Joseph and Jesus are the same name?"

"Yes, and Joshua. And Moses. It also suggests that Gikonyo, too, is a creator, a man with the kind of practical skills that a new nation will require. As the novel progresses we see that Mumbi is also a very practical person: she knits, prepares meals, and cares for her child; she helps her mother rebuild their home. Ngugi is setting these two up as characters that will play a very important role in the novel. A significant portion of *A Grain of Wheat* is made up of their separate confessions to Mugo, which has an unignorable bearing on the way the novel ends.

"Like the white missionaries, Kihika uses the Bible to justify his actions. He doesn't seem to be aware of this irony but Ngugi ensures that the reader is. Kihika is invoking Karl Marx's attitude to religion that it is the 'opium of the people' when he talks of the missionaries, quote: 'beseeching us to lay our treasures in heaven where no moth would corrupt them. But he laid his on earth, our earth.' The black people were betrayed by the white people – missionaries, soldiers, settlers – who promised to give but instead took. Imperialism with its practical application, colonialism, is the ultimate betrayer; and the novel is interwoven with almost countless minor betrayals. As General R hesitantly says, toward the end of the novel: 'You – no one will ever escape from his own actions.'

"The dangerous but historically necessary process of mythologising continues. People come to believe that Kihika could, quote: 'move mountains and compel thunder from heaven.'

"Kihika is captured and though his torture is described, it is qualified by the phrase, 'some say'. The people of Thabai have mixed feelings for Kihika; he is their hero, quote: 'the terror of the white man', but they will suffer terribly because of his actions, and many will resent him for this. Making dramatic use of the short paragraph, Ngugi ends the chapter on an ambiguous note, quote: 'The party, however, remained alive, and grew, as people put it, on the wounds of those Kihika left behind.' The sentence picks up the metaphor of the grain of wheat, with the Biblical implications that it might not grow straight – especially if the people resent their wounds because most of them just want to get on quietly with their domestic lives even under the yoke of colonialism. Notice how, once again, Ngugi shifts responsibility by saying 'as people put it'. Ngugi is not a polemicist; he is an artist, aware that nothing in life is certain, aware that words – especially in the language of the oppressor – cannot be taken for granted. The people of Kenya were betrayed by the white settlers; will they be betrayed again, by the party when it takes over in a few days' time. And that's about it."

"No wonder they jailed him."

"Who?"

"This Ngugi fellow."

" 'Those who tell the truth shall not escape whipping.'"

"'A dog's obeyed in office.'"

"You know your Shakespeare."

"Shakespeare, at least, can write."

"So can Ngugi."

"Now, Mr George, shall we get on with the second chapter?"

"That was the second chapter. You slept through the first. Check your Dictaphone!"

16

On his way back from prison, near Bradfield shopping centre, George was reminded that elections were imminent when a youth wearing a ZANU PF T-shirt handed him a flyer urging him to vote for 'Unity, Piss and Development'. He folded the newsprint and put it in one of his capacious khaki pockets. It would be useful for starting a fire.

He was anxious about the child. Was she safe? Had she had enough to eat? It was a long walk from Fife Street back to Hillside suburbs but it gave him the time he needed to decide on what was left of his future. That book was the key. On its title page, inscribed in orange crayon, were a name and an address: the name, Polly Petal, followed by the address, Empandeni Mission. He did not want to call her Polly Petal in case it was the name of some white child who had been the original owner of the book: a Ladybird edition of *The Enormous Turnip*, adapted by Fran Hunia from the traditional tale, and wonderfully illustrated by John Dyke – but when he mentioned the Mission to her, her face lit up and she smiled, really smiled, for the first time. This convinced George that the child's home was somewhere in Mpande Communal Land, and he was determined to return her to her people. He was going west, anyway, and this would give him a purpose.

His reveries were disturbed by a sudden hooting and a voice shouting, "Howzitt Sir!" George was walking along the cycle track on the left side of the road going out of town, and it was some distance from the parallel main road, but by squinting his eyes he managed to recognise, at the wheel of a purple Datsun 1200, none other than his old pupil McKaufmann, he who had got George into trouble on two counts: the Ian Smith photograph, and the unfortunate affinity, aurally, of his name with a racist insult. The car did a dangerous u-turn and screeched to a halt opposite George. "Jump in, Sir!" shouted McKaufmann, "We going for ice-cream at Eskimo Hut.

"I…"

"Ah come on, Sir, man; for old time's sake!"

"Well, all right; but I don't have any money." A back door opened and George squeezed in. McKaufmann was not alone. In the front passenger seat sat the androgynous City Lights, and in the back, sharing the cramped space with George, he didn't recognise them at first, were the twins, Helter and Skelter.

"Hullo, Sir," said Skelter, "how was prison?"

"Dreadful. But shouldn't you be at school?"

"Yes, but we decided to bunk out for a ice-cream. Mine's a choc fudge sundae."

"So's mine."

"And mine."

"Mine too."

"What about you, Sir?"

"I'm afraid I don't have any money."

"That's OK," said Helter.

"We'll stand you," said Skelter.

"It's very kind of you, boys. I'd like a lime-flavoured twirly cone." George was thinking of pre-Independence days, the sixties and seventies, when he and his friends paid regular visits to Eskimo Hut.

"I don't think they've got that kind any more," said City Lights.

"Well then, I'll have the same as you."

"Those are just about the most expensive."

"Oh," replied George, embarrassed, "then I'll have something cheaper."

"There's nothing cheap."

"Oh, well…"

Just before the turn-off to the Eskimo Hut there was a police road block. They were waved down by a woman wearing a yellow fluorescent jacket. McKaufmann gave the policewoman a friendly greeting. She walked round the car looking at whatever traffic police look at and stopped at the driver's window. "Please show me your licence."

"Certainly officer," said McKaufmann and, to George's amazement, he pulled a R100 note out of his shirt pocket and pressed it into the policewoman's hand.

She closed her fist over it and said quietly: "You can go."

"Thank you, officer," smiled Ivan Mckaufmann, "have a good day." Then he drove into the Eskimo Hut car park, and they all piled out.

"You sure you won't have something, Sir?"

"Quite sure, thank you; I had a huge breakfast in prison."

"What did you have?"

"Well, you can choose between continental and English. For continental they offer you fresh fruit juice, yoghurt, coffee or tea, and two fresh croissants with butter and apricot preserve."

"And for English?"

"For a full English you get two eggs, three rashers of bacon, a sausage, fried tomato and baked beans. You also get two slices of toast with butter and marmalade, and a choice of tea or coffee."

"You joking, aren't you man, Sir, man?"

"Well…"

"Don't you just get bread and water once a day?"

"In the books, you do. In real life it's not so bad."

"Old Crackling had to go to jail," said City Lights, spooning – well not quite spooning, since s/he was using a little flat plastic object – spatulating, shall we say, the ice-cream into his/her mouth.

"Yes,' said one of the twins, "he was caught trying to buy forex from Hove; you know his dad is high up in the police?"

"I believe so," said George disingenuously. "Now I'm going to have to leave you. I have certain duties to perform." George's knees creaked as he got up from the ground where they were sitting. His stomach ached. He dusted his shorts and returned his fez to his head.

"Sure we can't give you a lift back, Sir?"

"Quite sure, thank you." Deep down, he bristled at the fact that they had extended his walk by quite some distance. He swore silently at the little buggers. "Bye. Enjoy your chocolate fudge sundaes with an extra sprinkling of nuts!"

"Bye Sir. Enjoy your walk."

For a second time he passed the colony of white-browed sparrow-weavers. They had taken up residence in a buffalo thorn tree, also known as *haak en steek* (good name for Wilhelmine, thought George bitterly). One of the juveniles perched in the tree issued a warning and the birds, which had been foraging on the ground, flew up to safety. A peculiarity of these birds is that they build their nests on the side of the tree that faces the setting sun. George would use them to guide him to Empandeni Mission. He knew a bit about the place: that it was the oldest Catholic mission in Zimbabwe, originally set up by Jesuits under Father Prestage, and that it was located in an extremely drought-prone part of the country.

A few months ago George wouldn't have been able to walk more than a few metres in his bare feet. Now his soles were as hard as toenails. Paper thorns could not penetrate them, nor the heat of tarmacadam under a summer sun. Where he did suffer was round the sides of his feet as the hardened skin split, exposing raw flesh. He treated this condition with Vaseline petroleum jelly, panacea of the African poor. It was near a culvert, where he stopped to massage his heels, that George's sharp eye for food plants located a single cherry tomato bush fairly laden with fruit. He picked enough to half fill one of his pockets and then continued on his way.

The emergency taxi pick-up points were crowded with immaculately dressed people waiting for transport to and from town. Because of chronic fuel shortages very few taxis were running. One battered white Toyota minibus finally arrived at a point across the road from George, and he saw that the tout was hard-pressed to control would-be passengers. The sliding door must have been rusty because it couldn't open fully. Consequently a woman, broad in the beam, wearing a shocking pink slack-suit, so tight it made George's eyes water, got stuck. Some people tried to push her in and some tried to push her out. She began to scream very loudly. (George thought of the time Winnie-the-Pooh got stuck in a tight place: Rabbit's hole. He couldn't go on and he couldn't go back.) Eventually the in-pushers triumphed over the out-pushers, and a pink explosion momentarily lightened the drab interior of the taxi.

When George got home, tired out, Ajax and Hercules were overjoyed to see him. "Hush dogs, hush," he said. He didn't want the madam to know he'd got back before he could attend to the child, and get an hour's rest for himself. He approached his *khaya* with trepidation. There was no immediate sign of her. He had left the door unlocked because his only other option would have been to lock it, with her either inside or outside.

He had taught the dogs to ignore the child so his hope had been that she would be free to move and feel quite safe. He decided to look all round the *khaya* before going in, and it was on the leeward side where he built his fire, while peering into the plumbago hedge, that something attached itself to his khaki shorts, squashing a few cherry tomatoes in the process. It gave him a mild fright but when he turned around he discovered the child, alive and well. She was hugging him. He lifted her into his arms and danced round and round laughing, a little tearfully, and telling her what a brave girl she was. Then he set about making her something to eat: sadza with tomato, spinach, and mushroom relish seasoned with stolen salt and ground black pepper.

While they were waiting for the food to cook, George took the child in his lap and read her *The Enormous Turnip*, turning the pages very slowly so that she could enjoy the wonderful illustrations:

THIS OLD MAN HAS SOME TURNIP SEEDS. They lingered over the pictorial details: the old man with his myopic, demented eyes studying the seed packet, a rake gripped more like a weapon than a garden implement, in his left hand. He had a bushy moustache, which obliterated his top lip, and his bald head was shaped somewhat like the vegetable of his choice. His coat belt was buckled at the last notch, indicating quite a paunch. She pointed to the bird pecking in the prepared ground. It looked like a robin redbreast; then to the standing spade, the empty wooden box; then beyond to the broken stone wall, the gates, the sagging fence; then further away to the grassy hill, and trees in their autumnal shades. Whatever she pointed to he named or described, but he was never sure if she understood a word of it.

THE OLD MAN PLANTS THE SEEDS. This is a close-up. The old man is bent almost double. He has discarded the rake and in its place is a sturdy walking-stick. The bird is close to the furrow where he is dropping the seeds. It is this left hand which now holds on to the seed packet. His eye is almost popping out with the pressure of bending over. Is he warning the bird to stay away from his seeds, or has he become mesmerised by the circle of his thumb and forefinger? The margin along the fence is choked with grass and weeds ('Thistle and darnel and dock grew there').

HE WATERS THE SEEDS. The leaking watering can has an oversized rose with large holes. The outpour threatens to wash away the seeds. The old man has pushed a stick through the seed packet and stood it at the edge of the bed. His rake and his walking-stick are resting against the fence. There is a bucket of water behind him for refilling the watering can. His face has lost its demented look. He is almost serene.

"Right, my girl," said George, closing the book, lifting her off his lap, and preparing to get up, "it's time to eat. I'll read you a little more before we go to bed." He was dreading his encounter with Beauticious. She would scream at him for missing a day and half of work, and she would dock his pay accordingly. They were half way through their meal when it came.

"*Iwe*, Joji! Buya lapa checha! Wena! Intu! Mina hasi bulala wena! Fokkin mampara! Ipi wena konile?"

"Coming, madam, coming."

17

SALMAGUNDI

Talk about coincidences! George had dug out his copy of *The Matopos*, edited by Sir Robert Tredgold, K.C.M.G. It was a revised edition of 'A Guide to the Matopos' by Dr E.A. Nobbs (all those abbreviations), and had been published by The Federal Department of Printing and Stationery, 1956, the year George's little brother, Percy, had been born, and died. At the back of the book there was a fold-out map of the Matopos area, which, George hoped, might include the location of Empandeni Mission. Unfortunately it didn't extend that far, but there, at the western end of the Matopos, was his grandmother's birth place: Old Mangwe Fort. Empandeni Mission would be a few kilometres further west, close to the Botswana border. George felt an inexplicable surge of apprehension. He would visit the place where his family had begun, in 1896, the year of the first Chimurenga.

The fort had been built during the outbreak of the Matabele War in 1893. Its purpose was to guard the coach road that led to Bulawayo, the road along which the first whites had entered the land controlled by Mzilikazi, king of the warlike Matabele. First came the hunters, then the missionaries, then the traders. It was an underground fort, circular in structure, like a doughnut; only, where the hole should have been there was a column of earth and rock, which supported a roof made of Mopani poles and sand bags. After the Matabele War it was used as a storage facility for grain; consequently it became infested with vermin. It was to this sanctuary that about 150 settlers fled during the 1896 uprisings. There they suffered for many months, in constant fear of having their throats cut: the archetypal colonial nightmare. That the fort was never attacked is one of the more poignant ironies of Zimbabwean history. A voice from a cave in the Matopos gave orders to the warriors that the road to the south should be left open so that the settlers could run back to wherever they had come from. Instead it gave reinforcements, under the command of Plumer, free access to provide relief for the embattled white community. If it weren't for Mlimo, thought George with more sentiment than irony, I wouldn't be where I am today. The bastard!

In order to punish George for going to prison in her time, Beauticious arranged to hire him out for a wedding the following weekend. Normally he got a five per cent cut and he was allowed to keep any tips, but this time he would get no cut and he would have to surrender his tips. Fair is fair. I mean! Some months before, Beauticious had hired, for George to wear, an Elizabethan outfit, doublet and hose, from the theatre club. Among the *nouveau riche* of Zimbabwe there is a tacit understanding that what you hire or borrow you need not return; and Beauticious had no intention of returning the costume, or the various stuffed animals she had hired, through a contact of a contact of a contact (above board since they were all somehow related) from Bulawayo's Museum of Natural History. At least she didn't steal them, like those settler bastards who stole the soapstone Zimbabwe birds! Or those goffels who stole the gold cup that was presented every year at the Trade Fair to the farmer whose bull had the biggest balls! *Hokoyo!*

George had thus far performed at two weddings. It was his job to drive the car (the madam's blinded Wabenzi) which brought the bride and her pre-nuptial entourage to the church; thence the bride and her post-nuptial entourage (the groom squeezed in) to the fountain in the Centenary Park, for photographs. It was also his job to decorate the car with ribbons and balloons. Most important of all was the ceremony of opening the doors for the distinguished passengers. His anachronistic presence was an endless source of amusement for the guests – one man in his time plays many parts (not those 'parts', George!) – and how he hated it.

But it wasn't going to happen. George had other plans. Today was Sunday. He'd give the boys their last lesson on *King Lear*. The following day, Monday, he would go to work as usual (the Minister was back in town, *id est*, back in the madam's bed), and when the children were at school and the madam was enjoying her workout at Muscles and Curves, and the Minister was away doing what he did best: nothing… in-between preparing a delicious lamb curry, he would steal whatever was necessary for the journey to Empandeni Mission. He would walk out of this life, his precious charge by his side, very early on Tuesday morning. Fortunately he had marinated the two kilograms of stewing lamb before his arrest on Friday so only the slow cooking was necessary. He would keep the washing and the ironing to a minimum – he had rinsed his last thong. He was not going to over-exert himself on his final working day. It is a long walk to the place where the sun sets, and George's foetus was beginning to kick.

"You see, boys, old Lear, he's either in the court or on the heath. He can't connect the two."

"How do you mean, Sir?"

"The court represents ritual, order, art; the heath represents reality, disorder, nature. Lear rejects the court for the heath, which gives him insight into the court where 'robes and furred gowns hide all', but no metaphysical insight, no sense of the necessity of opposites, no realisation that the court *is* the heath, and the heath is the court. The German philosopher, Nietzsche called these opposites the Apollonian and the Dionysian. 'Contrariety,' he said, 'is the centre of the universe'. Take the colour orange. Its contrarieties are the colour gold and the colour red. Gold is a celestial colour. It is male. Red is a chthonic colour…"

"Thonic?"

"Of the earth. It is female. Lear sees either gold or red, never orange… except…"

"Except?"

"Except, perhaps, his duet with Cordelia, towards the end of Act Four, when he starts to emerge from profound unconsciousness… and there is soft music… and his head is upon his daughter's lap… Shall we read it? I'll do Lear. One of you, do Cordelia."

"I'll do it," said Helter, "I've got the place."

"OK. Start from, 'O, look upon me, sir'."

HELTER: O, look upon me, sir,

                    And hold your hands in benediction o'er me.

                    No, sir, you must not kneel.

GEORGE: Pray, do not mock me:

                    I am a very foolish fond old man.

110

Fourscore and upward, not an hour more nor less;
And, to deal plainly,
I fear I am not in my perfect mind.
Methinks I should know you and know this man;
Yet I am doubtful; for I am mainly ignorant
What place this is, and all the skill I have
Remembers not these garments, nor I know not
Where I did lodge last night. Do not laugh at me;
For as I am a man, I think this lady
To be my child, Cordelia.

HELTER: And so I am, I am.

GEORGE: Be your tears wet? Yes, faith. I pray, weep not.
If you have poison for me, I will drink it.
I know you do not love me; for your sisters
Have, as I remember, done me wrong.
You have some cause. They have not.

HELTER: No cause, no cause.

George put down his text and the twins were embarrassed to see tears in his eyes. He wiped them with the tassel on his fez and apologised for succumbing to Lear's penitence. He swallowed hard and began: "He remembers neither his garments (the court) nor where he lodged the night before (the heath). The contraries have merged, briefly, into music."

"Orange?"

"Catharsis. Read about it in the *Penguin Dictionary of Symbols*. There's a copy in the school library, or there used to be. Like all great symbols, it's a paradox (ho hum, George): it stands for divine love *and* lust, steadfastness *and* capriciousness. It is associated with Apollo and Dionysus, reason and emotion, linear time and cyclical time…"

"Sir?"

"Yes, my boy."

"Would you mind if we carried on reading the play? There's such a long way to go."

"Of course not. Sorry. I tend to get carried away. Where were we?"

"Act One, Scene 2, where Edmund says 'Thou, nature, art my goddess…'"

"Now there's an interesting word," said George. The twins sighed. "Nature. You see, what's natural on the heath is unnatural at court. At court it is unnatural for children to usurp their parent, but on the heath, red in tooth and claw, it's the most natural thing in the world. But if you see the court and the heath as the same place, a word like 'nature' becomes a paradox of a paradox of a paradox (Oh dear!)."

"Please, George, can we read?"

"Yes, but remember, Edmund is a 'natural' son; in other words a bastard, like Mlimo."

"Who?"

"What?"

"Nothing… er… let's read: 'Thou, nature, art my goddess; to thy law / My services are bound. Wherefore should I / Stand in the plague of custom…' now there's an interesting phrase, boys… let me explain to you the difference between primogeniture and tanistry. You see, in *Macbeth*…"

"We aren't doing *Macbeth*, we're doing *King Lear*, and we're running out of time."

"Can't we just read the play?"

"All right. Let's read it as a version of the Cinderella story. You know about Cinderella?"

"Yes, you told us to find out about her, but that's a fairy tale!"

"So is *King Lear*. Once upon a time there lived a foolish old king who had three daughters…"

Helter, then Skelter, stood up. "Sorry, Sir," said the former, "but I don't think you are helping us with this play." They mumbled some thanks and then wandered back to the house to watch videos and to enjoy pizza and Coca-Cola from the takeaway. George sighed with relief – he was in a lot of pain – and went into his *khaya* to see if the child was all right.

She was sitting on the bed in her red shirt and her blue jeans, bare feet crossed over so that her toes could play with each other, and she was paging through *The Enormous Turnip*. She looked up and smiled at George who offered her the roasted mealie the twins had brought. She took it gently and began to nibble away at the pips. "Shall we read a little before bed," said George. He took the book from her lap and sat down beside her. "Where were we? Ah, yes.

"THE TURNIP SEEDS GROW. The old man sits on a log watching the turnips grow. He has removed his coat so we can see that he is wearing a red shirt – just like yours – and a narrow grey waistcoat. His trousers are almost golden in that summer light. Between his splayed legs he leans contentedly on his walking-stick. Look, there's the bird, on the edge of the log, singing away merrily. She is not afraid of the old man. Notice: one of the turnips is already showing signs of being a lot larger than the others. Behind the old man there is a water pump painted green, and behind that, his thatched house with its tiny window and its huge chimney. I wonder who plays on that swing hanging from a branch of the stout oak tree…"

The little girl had begun to snore. The half-eaten mealie was still in her hand. George bent down and kissed her on the forehead; then he put the mealie on the box table and tucked her into bed. He went outside for a few minutes to gaze at the evening star.

18

A SENTENCE IS BUT A CHEV'RIL GLOVE...

"So George," said the minister, wiping egg from his moustache with one of George's grandmother's linen table napkins still in its ivory ring, "have you decided whom to vote for in the forthcoming elections?"

"I'm not allowed to vote, Master. My name disappeared from the voters' roll some years ago." George was busy clearing away breakfast things, keeping his head low. Beauticious was chatting to Titty on her cellphone. The children were finishing off with toast and marmalade. They were enjoying the imported butter the minister had brought with him.

"Well, what do you expect?"

"Master?"

"You whites – what do you expect? Weren't you offered the hand of friendship, by no less a personage than His Excellency, Robert Gabriel Mugabe?"

"We..."

"Do you remember his words, George? Cast your mind back to midnight, 17 April, 1980... 'If yesterday I fought you as an enemy, today you have become a friend. If yesterday you hated me, today you cannot avoid the love that binds me to you and you to me...'"

"'You to me and me to you'."

"What?"

"Er..."

"'Er who... er... whom?'"

"Master."

"That is better." The children crunched away on their toast and marmalade, sipping their coffee, which George had made from freshly ground beans. "And what did you do to that blessèd hand? You bit it, George, you bit it!"

"I'm sorry, master. Would you like some more coffee?"

"Yes. Fill her up. And George!"

"Master?"

"Give us a smile. There's nothing worse than a sullen servant." While he replenished the minister's cup, his mother's christening mug, George, by concentrating on the next day's journey westward, managed a real smile. "That's better. Here." The minister rummaged in a pocket of his Saville Row suit, and pulled out a fistful of money, which included, George couldn't help noticing, Euros, U.S. dollars, and rands. He selected a green $500,000 bearer's cheque and flicked it at George. "Buy yourself a small onion."

"Thank you, master." George put down his tray, picked up the note and put it in his pocket. He lifted the tray with its trembling crockery and cutlery, and turned towards the kitchen.

"Oh and George!" George paused on the threshold. "Back!"

George who had been feeling anaemic for some time, began to lose consciousness. He had a vague sense of the tray crashing to the ground; then he fell, it seemed, in slow motion. He was dimly aware of Beauticious screaming at him. He thought the children got up from their chairs half wanting, half afraid to go to his assistance... Ultimate, are you taking a step towards me? Madam's holding you back by the sleeve...

ULTIMATE: Let me go!

BEAUTICIOUS: Stay where you are!

THE MINISTER: Be careful! He's wicked (Helter and Skelter turn towards George.) With people of colour.

SKELTER: Is that him?

HELTER: (trying to remember the name) Er...

SKELTER: God, no!

HELTER: Yes.

MINISTER: I present myself: Gonzo.

VLADIMIR: (to Estragon) Not at all!

ESTRAGON: He said Godot.

VLADIMIR: Not at all.

ESTRAGON: (timidly to the minister) You're not Mr Godot, Sir?

115

MINISTER: (terrifying voice) I am Gonzo! (silence) Gonzo! (silence) Does that name mean nothing to you, nothing to you, nothing…

As George started coming round, the literary world faded and the real world re-focused. Beauticious was shouting at him in fanakalo, the children were in their rooms getting ready for school, and the minister was talking on his cellphone to one of his mistresses. "Fokkin sheet! Wena bataal zonke lo indaba lapa mathings ka mina! Iswili! I said ISWILI!"

"Yes, Madam. *Ngiaxolisa.*"

"Don't you dare speak to me in the vernacular, boy! Cheeky so-and-so." And with that she knocked his fez off his head with a hand full of rings the size of knuckle-dusters.

George sighed with relief when, at last, he had the house to himself. He had marinated the lamb in white wine and yoghurt; now he prepared to transform it into his favourite dish, though these days he had almost no appetite for any kind of food. He dusted the meat with flour, and browned the pieces in a large iron pot, which was already simmering with chopped onion and garlic. He added the curry powder, medium strength, and mixed it in. He added more white wine to prevent burning.

While he worked George recalled his forty years as a school teacher, first in 'fascist' Rhodesia, then in 'Marxist' Zimbabwe. He calculated that if he subtracted his years away at university in South Africa, he would have spent twenty-eight years as a Rhodesian and twenty-eight years as a Zimbabwean. Politically the times had been not so different. The nicest people in both eras, George reflected, had been the poor and the little children, especially those from the rural areas. What is it that turns people ugly when their aspirations to acquire property, to climb on the gravy train, are fulfilled? Is money so addictive that the more you get, the more you want? Why do people like Beauticious strive to out-Rhodie the Rhodies? Their churches, their social gatherings have been replaced by shopping malls… (all right, George, that's quite enough moralising for one day!).

He added the cumin seeds, the coriander (leaves and seeds), the cinnamon sticks, the clove, the bay leaf, the aniseed, the mustard seeds, the fresh chopped ginger, the curry bush leaves, the tamarind, the coconut milk, the cardamom seeds (take it easy, George!), stirring the while with a wooden spoon. Then he added a couple of pints of his own vegetable stock made from carrots, onions, celery, bouquet garni, a touch of horse radish, butter, pepper and salt, and left it to cook ever so slowly. He would prepare the basmati rice and the salads shortly before serving dinner.

There's no communication, thought George. The sentence with its binary structure, subject/predicate, has failed us. We can build computers but we can't love our neighbours, let alone our enemies. We don't know how to tell them. While he washed the breakfast things his mind wandered to a lesson he had attempted to give to a form four class on sentence awareness.

"Hush, boys and girls, hush! Rudo, stop that! James, no! Please, Thembani? Miriam!" Gradually the pandemonium would settle into a dull roar, above which George would attempt to pitch his lesson. There were always a handful of conscientious students who resented the fact that George couldn't control the class. He was a chalk and talk type teacher, which meant frequently having to turn your back, and that was when the missiles flew. "All right, then, who can define a sentence?" Smart Alec (his actual name!) puts up his hand. George's heart sinks. "Yes, Smart."

"It's what comes between a capital letter and a full stop, Sir."

"Well, yes… you're quite right."

"Put it this way, Sir, I'm not wrong. Litotes."

"Er… yes. That's – who threw that rubber?"

"Don't you mean condom, Sir?"

"That's enough, Lertitia! That… er… eraser. Who threw it?"

"Sir, you criticise us for using sound wobbles in our writing; now you are using one!'

"I am?"

"Yes. 'who threw' – that's a sound wobble."

"So it is… you two (oops, another one) stop pinching each other. I said stop it! Now Smart, your definition reminds me of Anthony Burgess' definition of a word: 'what comes between two spaces'; witty but not very helpful."

"Sir."

"Yes, Sabina."

"A sentence is a complete statement."

"Now that's a pretty good definition. Let's test it on the opening sentence of your set work, *Lord of the Flies*. Who brought their books with them?" About six hands went up. "I did ask you to bring both your novels to this lesson. OK, those with books, look (oops) at the first sentence; the rest of you LISTEN UP!" The shouting sometimes worked for a few seconds. "Please read it, Sabina?"

"'The boy with fair hair lowered himself down the last few feet of rock and began to pick his way towards the lagoon.'"

"Thank you. This may be called a compound sentence because it is made up of two simple sentences, which are joined by the word 'and'. We could re-write it – Farai, behave yourself! – 'The boy with fair hair lowered himself down the last few feet of rock, full stop. He began to pick his way towards the lagoon.' Now we have two complete statements, two simple sentences.

"Golding's second complete statement (or sentence) is: 'Though he had taken off his school sweater and trailed it, now from one hand, his grey shirt stuck to him and his hair was plastered to his forehead.' This may be called a complex sentence because the main clause, 'His grey shirt stuck to him and his hair was plastered to his forehead' is joined by a subordinate clause introduced by the conjunction 'though'." After about ten minutes of a lesson, George would kind of automatise, go on with what he had prepared regardless of interruptions, even ones that stung his face or stained his safari suit.

"It's actually more than a complex sentence; it's a compound-complex sentence since it also contains the conjunction 'and' (twice). We could re-write it, 'He had taken off his school sweater, full stop. He trailed it now from one hand, full stop. His grey shirt stuck to him, full stop. His hair was plastered to his forehead. Now we have four complete statements, four simple sentences. But see how it has altered Golding's style!"

He wiped a piece of spit-soaked toilet paper off his forehead. He should have taken an example from a simpler text – the Ladybird series would have been more appropriate for that bunch! As he swept and dusted, swept and dusted, he re-created his lesson… Embedding incorporates the three ways of constructing a sentence: simple, compound, and complex. Sometimes short sentence clusters can be improved by embedding them into a single coherent sentence. Let's take an example from *The Gingerbread Boy* (George imagined writing on the chalk board):

> The little old woman mixed the gingerbread. She cut out the little boy's head. She cut out his body. She cut out his arms. She cut out his legs. She patted them out flat. She placed them on a baking tin.

Now, this is how the Ladybird Books' writer embedded the sentence clusters:

> So the little old woman mixed the gingerbread. She cut out the little boy's head, his body, his arms and his legs. She patted them out flat on a baking tin.

Seven sentences have become embedded into three sentences. It's my turn to embed the three into one:

> After mixing the gingerbread, the little old woman cut out the little boy's head, his body, his arms and his legs; then she patted them out flat on a baking pan.

How did I do it? By using a technique called subordination, I created one complex sentence. I used two subordinating conjunctions, 'after' (temporal) and 'then' (temporal). There are five categories of subordinators and the clauses they introduce: temporal, causal, circumstantial, spatial, relational... words, words, words, said Hamlet to Polonius; sword, sword, sword. I will speak daggers...

The fragrance of curried lamb pervaded his nostrils as he dusted and swept, made the beds, collected the dirty washing, removed the empty sweet and crisp packets, switched off lights... chore after chore. Housework was back-breaking. He didn't want to leave any suggestion of a possible change of plan in his life. The slightest oversight in his routine would make Beauticious suspicious (oops, another sound wobble). She loved, for instance, to check for dust by wiping her finger along the mantelpiece, or the top of a wardrobe. Or she'd hold a glass up to the light and check for fingerprints or lip marks. If she found a fault she would dock George's wages. No, on this, his last day, George would leave the house spick and span. The neglected washing would not be noticed for a couple of days.

Now was the time to steal a few basic necessities for the journey to the child's home. Into his hands went a box of matches, a cruet of salt and pepper mixed (the cruet had been part of a set he had given his mother and father on their twenty-fifth wedding anniversary) a tube of Betadine antiseptic cream, a serrated knife (part of a set of steak knives he had given to his parents one Christmas), a handful of tea leaves, a bag of mealie meal, and one of the children's numerous, never used, backpacks. Into the last named went the loot, and into the dustbin, for the time being, went the last named. Before fetching the children from school (Beauticious made a point of never being there when they got home – all that fuss) George would steal a little of the curry for the child. He wanted her to have a nourishing meal before they set out on their adventure.

The rest of George's long working day passed off uneventfully. The backpack had been removed without detection to his *khaya*, the child had been stuffed with protein and was fast asleep in his arms. He was sitting by the fire, the dogs next to him, listening to the sounds of the night. His now chronic stomach pain had been eased a little by the mug of tea he was sipping, and he thought of his one-way conversation with the Minister of Child Welfare, Sweets and Biscuits, and where the coming elections would place that gentleman in the capricious world of power-mongering. He remembered how eagerly he had purchased and read, shortly after Independence, the biography of Robert Mugabe by the English journalists, David Smith and Colin Simpson. He still possessed that copy and now, by the light of a candle supplemented by the fire, he strained his eyes to re-read the last page, wondering at the ironies of time and circumstance:

> The man himself remains as committed as ever to the principles he outlined to the UN General Assembly when he made his debut there last September.
>
> 'When ZANU ascended to power we felt the moment demanded of us a spirit of pragmatism, a spirit of realism, rather than that of emotionalism, a spirit of reconciliation and forgiveness rather than that of vindictiveness and retribution. We had to stand firm to achieve total peace rather than see our nation sink to the abyss of civil strife and continued war … we had to embrace one another in the spirit of our one nationality, our common freedom and independence, our collective responsibility.'

About the same time Mugabe was asked how he, the psychopathic killer, the ogre, the terrorist of yesterday, had become the pragmatist, the moderate, the statesman of today. His reply was a testament to himself as man and politician. 'The change,' he said, 'is not in me. I am not the one who has undergone a metamorphosis. The transformation really is taking place in the minds who once upon a time regarded me as an extremist, a murderer, a psychopathic killer … they are the people who have had to adjust to the change. I have remained my constant self. What I was, I still am.'

Whether Mugabe can remain his constant self in the face of the crises that await him is an open question.

'His dilemma is that if he takes too much away from the whites they will leave.

'But if he gives too little to the blacks they will revolt.'

That, in the words of a British diplomat who had worked with him at Lancaster House and during the election, was the tightrope he had to tread after independence.

It is a tightrope he has to keep walking. A dilemma that cannot be solved until he has won the economic freedom that only the whites can give him.

No one should doubt his commitment, only whether he can buy himself enough time.

George poured the dregs of his tea on the fire. The embers hissed. Gently he stood up and moved into his room. He tucked the child up in bed. He dug around in his box table and withdrew a large manila envelope. It contained the papers that gave him his identity: his birth certificate, his academic and professional qualifications, his redundant will, his expired passport, his vehicle licence, and his National Registration card. (His deceased pets' papers were also in there.)

He returned to the fire, placed the envelope on the rosy glow of Mopani wood, and waited for it to burst into flames. Afterwards he killed the fire by urinating on it – all that tea. Then he went to bed.

19

LONG DAY'S JOURNEY

Ajax and Hercules knew something was amiss. Both had begun to whine like puppies. George was wondering whether to go barefoot like the little girl, sockless in his tackies, or socked (Woolworths) in his Chinese-made reinforced cardboard shoes. He decided on the first option. The soles of his feet were now hard enough to withstand most obstacles. The rest of his attire was the familiar khaki shirt and shorts, and red fez with its somewhat worn tassel. With the added bottle of water and the relish pot, his stolen backpack was packed (that's not a wobble, George, it's a crash!). He slipped it on and adjusted the straps for a comfortable fit. He held out his hand to the little girl and together they walked away. The dogs, whimpering, accompanied them to the side gate, where George and Joseph had first seen the child lying on her tummy on the road, waiting for the next car to take her even further away from her rural home than Bulawayo. George hugged the dogs, told them to hush, held back a tear, and lifted the child and himself over the gate.

There was no moonlight but the Milky Way – dominated by the giant hunter of Boeotia, his belt so polished that George could detect, by its light, a predominance of yellow blossom along Leander Avenue – the Milky Way guided the travellers:

A broad and ample road, whose dust is gold
And pavement stars, as stars to thee appear,
Seen in the galaxy – that Milky Way,
Thick, nightly, as a circling zone, thou seest
Powdered with stars.

Crikey, Milton is heavy going! It was tecoma, mostly, but also cassia, the buttercup tree, smelling of fruit followed by scrambled eggs on toast. In the thick foliage of the syringas, bunches of bright green berries gleamed, berries light enough to sting but not damage the flesh of playground children in another place and another time.

122

They crossed Hillside Road. The child pointed out clumps of tithonia, no longer in their prime, in the culverts and under the bougainvillea hedges; and lavender tinted convolvulous, trailing along, under, and over everything. George had heard somewhere that you could extract pounds, shillings and pence from the seeds of these lovely flowers. They passed the Church of Ascension where George's parents had been joined together in holy matrimony, where he and his brother had been christened, and where Mom, Dad, and little Percy had, in his or her time, been given a solemn send-off. They walked briskly, filling their lungs with cool, woodsmoke-scented air. The cocks had not yet begun to crow, not even the high-pitched Toyota from what was once next door. At Matopos Road they turned left and walked along it until, just after Napier, they entered the Old Gwanda Road. Here the smells became more competitive: a burst sewerage pipe was contending for dominance with a grove of eucalyptus trees. The verges on either side of the road were teeming with grasses of every variety, testimony to a good rainy season, and a bankrupt municipality.

Where Tait Road begins, they picked up their first scent of the bush beyond: the acacia Karroo was beginning to flower. And then, George's heart swelled with nostalgia when he detected the first farmyard smells: dung and silage mingled with threshed corn. Suddenly the road was littered with bits of chewed-and-spat sugar-cane. As they passed Knott's Way, and then Circular Drive, the houses thinned out considerably, and there was a reassuring presence of real bush. Fine thatching grass began to dominate the space on either side of the road, but it could not conceal the stench of household rubbish – wealthy household rubbish. This was Bulawayo's prime area for the extremely large, ostentatiously designed 'small houses', which the chefs of Zimbabwe – businessmen, criminals, and senior civil servants – were providing for their mistresses.

At the point where the tarred road ended and the dirt road began, there was a bottle store called Bagwale, on the right, and a sign to CHESA FORESTRY RESEARCH, on the left. The odd couple kept walking. They had not yet seen a single human being. George wanted to be well away from town before first light. The little girl showed no signs of tiring, and George was in reasonable spirits despite the tearing pain in his stomach. He now thought of her as Polly Petal, though he did not speak it. The dirt road was predominantly of dolerite, which made it very stony. For the first time George regretted not bringing shoes. His heavy heel came down on a particularly sharp piece of basalt and, from then on, he limped.

The stars lost their focus as the world began to lighten from the east. Now they could pick out the silhouettes of the scattered agaves, some looking like gigantic asparaguses, others, about to flower, like Victorian hatstands: African Christmas trees! They saw their first euphorbia, or *naboom*, as the Afrikaners call it. It reminded George of a pain even worse than that which he was feeling more and more frequently in his bowels. It had been somewhere in the West Nicholson area. His father, an amateur prospector, was wandering about dry river beds looking for gold-bearing quartz reefs. George was wandering, bored stupid, in his father's wake. He held a dried stick in his hands and used it to prod things living and things dead. He made the mistake of prodding a euphorbia branch, and some of its milky sap splashed into his left eye. Immediately the poison got to work on his mucous membranes, and the agony was so intense that he dropped to the hot sandy river bed and writhed there like a worm on the end of a hook. His father knew a doctor in Colleen Bawn about twenty kilometres away but by the time George had been treated with anaesthetic eye drops, the original pain had subsided to a bearable level. The doctor, also an amateur prospector with more quartz samples than medicines in his brown bag, told them that the local people used the euphorbia sap as a fish poison, and they called it *umhlonhlo*.

George's plan was that they would walk at night and early morning, and rest – hide – during the day, until they were far enough away from possible search parties. At the first sight of humanity, he would find a safe shady place in dense bush, cook a meal and then try to sleep. As the dawn chorus began, he listened for the sound of sparrow-weavers but heard only bulbuls and drongos and rattling cisticolas and … what was that distant sound? Not a bird, surely? A diesel engine. Then he saw the lights. He lifted his companion and carried her off a little way into the bush taking care not to become mired in the stinking containers of imported goods: bottles, cartons, cans, jars, tubes, tins, sachets and wrappers. The dense grass covering made the going difficult but once, just in time, he had crossed the verge, the real bush was relatively easy to navigate. He ducked as a Toyota Land Cruiser went rumbling by. They returned to the road, George put Polly down, and they resumed a brisk walking pace. George wanted to reach the Mzingwane River, beyond Mzilikazi's memorial, before it was too dark to dig for water. Any surface water at this time of year would be too risky.

Once there was enough light for him to see quite well, George searched the bush on either side for any form of nourishment. He was soon rewarded by the incongruous presence of a grove of prickly pears standing in the ruins of an abandoned shack. There were still some healthy looking fruits on the flattened stems. He pointed these out to Polly and she seemed to recognise them. He used the hard covers of *The Enormous Turnip* to protect his hands from the sharp spines, each one surrounded by terrible skin-piercing hairs. He closed the book on a fruit, twisted it off and then dropped it onto a sandy bit of ground. In this way he picked five fruits. Polly watched him intently as he rubbed each fruit in the sand using the thick leaves of a resident kalanchoe to protect his fingers. When the spines and the hairs had been removed he rummaged in his backpack and brought out the serrated knife. He made two or three incisions down the length of a fruit and then peeled them. The skin came off easily. He gave the first one to Polly who ate it with obvious pleasure. He ate the next one and was very pleased with its sweet juiciness, though he had no appetite for it. "You know," he said, speaking for the first time in hours, "my grandmother made prickly pear syrup. We used to eat it with our porridge in the mornings. It was delicious." One by one, he peeled and fed the three other fruits to her. "All those pips," he said, "they can constipate you." They returned to the road and went on their way.

After another hour or so the brave little girl began to show signs of fatigue. George's back was occupied so he scooped her over his fez and then settled her on his shoulders. She giggled when he pretended to gallop like a donkey. He secured her by the ankles and, in this way they continued their journey until shortly after sunrise. A woman was coming down the road ahead of them. She was expertly peeling and chewing a length of sugar-cane. The presence of another human being decided George. Time to find a place to rest. They had recently passed Mzilikazi's old kraal, Mhlahlandela, and George knew that they were not far from the Mzingwane River or a tributary of it. He left the road before the woman could take in any details of the apparition approaching her, and began to make his way through the bush.

He began to hum an old Paul Robeson song: 'Just a wearying for you' (for whom, Georgy boy?), and he felt the child relaxing into sleep. Her head came down on his fez and pushed it awry. Her breathing became heavy. 'All the time a-feeling blue.' Lest she fall, George lifted her off his shoulders and cradled her in his arms. She was growing heavier by the minute. Where's that darn river? 'Wishing for you, wond'ring when…' Paul dropped his Gs but George preferred to retain them. In real life Paul Robeson, one of George's few heroes, spoke immaculate English, but in song a certain stereotyping was expected of your negro. That wasn't the case, however, with 'Ol' Man River'. Robeson changed the words 'you get's a little drunk' to 'you show a little grit', and the song became a rallying cry for oppressed people all over the world. George once possessed (a few hours before) nearly every recording Paul Robeson had ever made… 'you'll be coming home again'… ah, Mina.

He found a sandy spruit and walked along it till he came to a pod mahogany still in full leaf surrounded by smaller trees and bushes. Under the canopy of the tree the spruit broadened into an acceptable resting place. George deposited the sleeping child on a level piece of ground and made a pillow for her with his old tracksuit top. He had packed it because the early mornings were turning chilly. He began scouting the area for kindling and firewood. From a distance came the sound of cow bells, and a little closer, the haunting call of a Cape turtle dove. It was going to be a hot day. Once he had collected enough fuel he made a fire-place further down the spruit; then he lay down beside the child and tried to sleep.

When he opened his eyes she was sitting next to him, holding out the book. "Let's see now," he said, "where did we get up to?" He took the book and opened it to the next page. "Here we are:"

ONE TURNIP GROWS AND GROWS AND GROWS! Isn't it huge? Look: its leaves are taller than the lower branches of the oak tree. Isn't the old man pleased with himself, the way he sticks his thumbs into his waistcoat pockets? Where's the little bird?

IT IS ENORMOUS! There's the bird! She's standing on the surface of the turnip, looking down in amazement. The turnip is taking up most of the picture. Where's the old man?

THE OLD MAN SAYS, I WANT SOME TURNIP FOR DINNER. There he is, indoors, bossing his poor wife around. His assertive hands with their hairy knuckles are in complete contrast to her submissive hands, clasped as if begging for mercy. He sits at a wooden table drinking his tea with the teaspoon still in the cup; but his plate is empty. Can you see his walking-stick? His ear looks inflamed. Hers are tucked away in her yellow bonnet. I don't like this picture much, do you? Let's turn over.

HE GOES TO PULL UP THE ENORMOUS TURNIP. He is wearing his coat. It must be getting chilly. He sits on a stool in order to pull on his boots. See the little mouse watching him from a hole in the wainscot. The door is open and we can look into the garden. The turnip looks smaller but that is because it is further away. It's an illusion of an illusion; and Plato would add another illusion. Nothing is, but what it seems to be.

There was a rustling sound in the grass nearby, and George closed the book. Both of them tensed, waiting. "Footsteps," whispered George, "someone is coming." He manoeuvred himself in front of the child. First one, then two, then three young men came into view in the clearing created by the spruit, about ten metres below them. George's stomach tightened with fear, a counter-irritant to his constant pain. They were dressed the way poor young men in Zimbabwe dress: tattered long-sleeved shirts with unbuttoned cuffs and untucked tails, shabby long trousers, and home-made sandals, or *amanyathelo*. Each one carried something in his right hand. Stones, thought George, to bludgeon me.

Then George noticed something that gave him hope. They were not looking directly at him – a sign of respect. He hailed them in Ndebele and they responded. The first youth came up to George (he could feel the child cowering against his back), placed his left hand under his right and laid the stone on the ground. But it wasn't a stone; it was an *ikhomane*, a delicious vegetable marrow, indigenous to Matabeleland. The second youth repeated this ritual with a spiny wild cucumber; the third, they looked like brothers, offered a glass bottle of fresh milk. George was overwhelmed. He asked them why, and the first youth, reverting to English, said they could see he was in trouble, and since he was on their father's land, it was customary for them to help him. George thanked them profusely and asked if they could rest there a little while longer. He was assured that he could stay and that he and the little girl would come to no harm. They saw her peeping at them over George's shoulder. Then they saluted George and walked away along the spruit. The companions lay down next to each other on the sand and promptly fell asleep.

20

INTO NIGHT

When they awoke, more or less at the same time, the sun was hovering on the horizon: a red balloon attached to a string of glowing clouds. George was in such pain that he needed to vomit; but he did not want to distress Polly. He crawled a way down the spruit and, where it turned a corner, brought up a mess of blood, bile, and prickly pear. After that he felt better, strong enough to prepare a meal.

He dug in the backpack for the box of matches and a few newsprint fliers. These he scrunched into balls and placed under the kindling on his makeshift stove. He lit the paper, blew gently on the flame, and once the kindling caught fire, added the heavier wood. Out came the pot, the Mazoe Orange bottle of water, the salt and pepper. First he offered the bottle to Polly who took a swig. Then he half-filled the pot and set it on the fire to boil. He added some salt and pepper and the *ikhomane*.

As the water began to warm, then steam, then simmer, then boil, the sun slowly sank, leaving the world in twilight, the crepuscular time. George's sense of loss was always more acute at this mystical time (not mystical, though, for the rabbits who came out of their warrens to eat, and got eaten, by any number of predators). The dying George thought of the dying Keats, his last letters to Charles Brown, as he lay in quarantine or in his tiny room above the Spanish Steps in Rome, listening to that incessant fountain. 'Here lies one whose name was writ in water.' He was dying not just of consumption but of unrequited love. It was his stomach, not his lungs, which pained him.

My dear Brown, I should have had her when I was in health, and I should have remained well. I can bear to die – I cannot bear to leave her. Oh, God! God! God! Every thing I have in my trunks that reminds me of her goes through me like a spear. The silk lining she put in my travelling cap scalds my head. My imagination is horribly vivid about her – I see her – I hear her. There

is nothing in the world of sufficient interest to divert me from
her a moment... Oh, Brown, I have coals of fire in my breast.

"Me too," George mused aloud, his arm around the little girl, his eyes
on the fire, "I always made an awkward bow."

He pushed the point of the serrated knife into the marrow but it was
not yet cooked. He peeled the wild cucumber and fed it to Polly in thick,
juicy slices. "You can have the milk with your sadza. Do you know, dear
child, that the troubadours of twelfth century Europe regarded amor as
the profoundest spiritual experience? And it didn't exist before they
brought it into being through song and poetry. There was only sexual desire or eros, and compassion or agape. The former is a biological urge, the
latter a spiritual urge. These can be seen as opposite kinds of love. What
happens, my dear, when opposites merge? You get a paradox (oh no!), a
third force, which transcends the two opposites, and the third force in this
case, is amor or romantic love." Polly was listening, not to the sense of
George's words, but to the reassuring sound of his voice – as the light
thickened. "Now paradoxes are notoriously unstable; they keep slipping
back into their opposite components, then merging again, slipping back,
and so on. So the transcendent experience is evanescent, passing... as it
comes it goes, like twilight." These were Joseph Campbell's ideas. What
was it that George wanted to look up in one of his books? Oh yes, the
corn myth. Too late now.

When the marrow was ready George speared it out with the knife,
rested it on some pod mahogany leaves, and added the mealie meal to the
now greenish boiling water. He stirred it briskly with a piece of driftwood, and continued stirring, adding a little more salt and pepper, until
it was ready to eat. He took the pot off the flames and added most of the
milk to it. Supper was ready. Polly ate ravenously but George could not
touch a thing. George scraped the left-over food into the ice-cream con-
tainer. He used some sand and a little of the water to scour the pot; then,
with a little more of the water, he rinsed it. He put it back on the fire and
poured in enough water for tea. As soon as the water started to boil he
added some tea leaves, let it boil a little longer, and took it off the stove.
He let it cool for a while then poured in the rest of the milk. George took
the first sip; he didn't want Polly to burn herself. "That's better," he said,

and he passed the pot to her. In this manner they shared the tea until they'd both had enough. Then it was time to continue their journey.

For another half hour there was sufficient light for George to lead the way, but when it got too dark for his eyes, Polly took over and walked in front of him. She seemed to know instinctively what direction to take, and her eyes were sharp enough to avoid the tough yellow trip lines of the ubiquitous golden orb-web spiders. A crescent moon made its appearance, the breeze turned gusty, and then a sound broke the silence, which froze the marrow in George's bones. It could have been the whoops, groans, grunts, whines, yells, cackles, giggles of one of his classes in session, Form 3 Remove in particular, with McKaufmann conducting; but it wasn't; it was a hyaena, *crocuta crocuta*. Polly looked back at him with enquiring eyes, and he forced a smile. "Keep going, little one; we must be close to the river. 'Old man river,'" he quietly sang, "'that old man river… he must know something… but don't say nothing… he just keeps rolling… he keeps on rolling… a… long'."

Indeed the river was close. They arrived at a spot about ten metres wide with two or three standing pools of water. Again the hyaena, *impisi*, called, and it too was close, closer than before. George's plan had been to dig for fresh water in order to re-fill the Mazoe Orange bottle, and then to continue on their way in what he hoped was the direction of Empandeni Mission. But now he couldn't risk it. He had heard too many stories of children being taken by these vicious creatures, and eaten alive. A friend of his, out camping, had been dragged from his tent by a female spotted hyaena. She bit off his knee and he had to have his leg amputated. In the middle of the widest part of the river bed, he began to build the biggest fire of his life. He knew he mustn't panic because that would be communicated to the child, and he wouldn't know how to deal with hysteria. She seemed cheerful enough as she helped him collect first the plentiful driftwood in the vicinity, and then, a little, just a little, further afield, along the banks, and deeper into the bush, all the firewood they could carry.

George's hands shook as he wasted a few precious matches, trying to get the flames going, but he managed, and when it was positively roaring, he felt more relaxed. Shielding the child, first with stacked firewood, and then with his legs and his arms, he sat as close to the blaze as possible. He scanned the surrounding bush but saw nothing. He had placed the end of a particularly long and stout piece of wood in the flames. If the worst came to the worst this would be his weapon of defence. Thank you, Prometheus, for giving us the gift of fire. Sorry you had to lose your liver in the process.

He smelt them before he saw them, and he saw them, first through Polly's eyes. Was it only hyaenas that she stared at, or were they being ridden by witches out to get a meal of human flesh and blood? He counted four pairs of eyes, each eye a miniature inferno. He put more wood on the fire. From a literary point of view (go on, George, we're listening!) these creatures recall the human fascination with hermaphroditism in which two opposites are combined (don't tell us; it's a paradox!). Recall that scene when Cassio calls Desdemona 'perfection':

CASSIO: She's a most exquisite lady.

IAGO: And I'll warrant her full of game.

CASSIO: Indeed she is a most fresh and delicate creature.

IAGO: What an eye she has! Methinks it sounds a parley to provocation.

CASSIO: An inviting eye, and yet methinks right modest.

IAGO: And when she speaks, is it not an alarum to love?

CASSIO: She is indeed perfection.

On Shakespeare's stage the female parts were played by boys, so Desdemona – a boy dressed as a girl, would be Hermes joined to Aphrodite…

Sir, Sir!

Yes, Farai.

Is that where aphrodisiac comes from?

Well, yes…

Sir, Sir!

Yes, Rudo.

What do you call a black script writer for children's movies?

I give up, what?

An Afrodisneyhack.

Ha ha, very funny. Now where was I? Adam and Eve were one before they separated – fell – into two. They were joined at the rib.

Sir, Sir!

Yes, Mustafah.

My dad says if you say anything bad about the Holy Koran he's going to come and fix you.

But this is the Bible, and…

Abraham is in the Bible!

I know, but…

Sir, can't you just give us notes? We going to fail our exams.

Circumcision has its origins in the idea that in the beginning we were one, both male and female.

Ah jeez, Sir!

The clitoris is what survives in the woman as a penis, so in order to make her fully a woman, it is removed. The foreskin is what survives in the man as a vulva, so in order to make him fully a man, it is removed. Now…

Sir, what's this got to do with Orthello, man?

The hyenas were circling them, and the circle was growing ever smaller; so was the pile of firewood. George's backside had made quite a dent in the river sand as he turned and turned to face the clan. Polly was starting to show signs of panic, so he dug *The Enormous Turnip* out of the backpack, and opened it on her lap.

HE PULLS AND PULLS, BUT HE CAN'T PULL UP THE ENORMOUS TURNIP. Just look at that crazy old man straining to unearth the turnip. His eyes are almost popping out of his head. Did you know, my love, that turnips are very good for you? And you shouldn't throw away the leaves because they are full of nutrition. The Italians use the roots in a rice dish called risotto; the Japanese pickle them; the French serve them with duck; I enjoy them in a good old Irish stew.

THE OLD MAN CALLS TO THE OLD WOMAN. COME AND HELP ME TO PULL UP THIS ENORMOUS TURNIP, HE SAYS. He hasn't been able to budge that turnip. See, the old woman has been hanging clothes – looks like underwear – on the washing line. She seems slightly less demented than her hus-

Polly's scream jerked him away from the text. The large female leader had broken the circle and was within snapping distance of George's feet. He pulled a brand from the fire and threw it in the hyaena's face. It grunted and retreated, baring its terrible yellow fangs. Those jaws that could snap bones as if they were soup crackers. George stood up, straddling the child, and, with the long burning piece of wood in his hands, began to shout defiance at the drooling carnivores. He might have been shouting at his pupils. It seemed to encourage them to advance, giggling and whooping. He groped about for more wood, one last piece, which he flung on the dying fire. It released a few sparks. One of the creatures made a swoop for the child who was clinging to George's legs. George lunged at it with the brand, and it retreated a little way. Now two of them approached, from opposite directions. Screaming curses, George swung the wood round and round. A third slunk in and took away the backpack. The female leader was inches from the little girl's head when shots rang out. She somersaulted and then lay still. The other three disappeared into the night. George's skinny legs buckled and he sank into his khaki shorts. Before losing consciousness he took the child in his arms and held her tightly.

When George came round, the first words he heard were, "Yes, Mabuku!"

"Ndiweni, is it you?"

"It is I, Mabuku."

"You are in uniform."

"National Parks. Anti-poaching unit." He let George inspect his battered AK47, a relic of the War of Liberation.

"You saved our lives. We are very grateful to you, Ndiweni."

"You are welcome. I am not forgetting that you bailed me out of prison."

"How is… er…"

"Dhlamini?"

"Yes."

"He is well. Isn't it, he has gone back to his village in Tsholotsho. He campaigns for Simba Makoni. What are you doing here Mabuku?"

George explained to his erstwhile cell mate that he was on his way to the Mangwe area to find the child's relatives. Ndiweni offered to accompany them to a safe spot in the Matopos National Park. It was part of the area he patrolled. They found the backpack, undamaged, a few metres from the fireplace. Apparently the hyaenas had escaped from one of the conservancies in the area. Ndiweni showed George the tag on the dead creature's left ear. He walked ahead with Polly and George following, George almost doubled up with stomach pain.

It was hours before they arrived at Nswatugi cave near Maleme Dam. Ndiweni had carried the child for the last few kilometres. He had also refilled their bottle with fresh water. He left the couple there after bidding them a warm farewell. They fell asleep under the polychrome giraffes, which had been painted by the aboriginal people of this land, how many thousand years ago?

21

WESTERING

When George opened his eyes Polly was already awake, examining the
paintings on the wall of the cave. She seemed to be particularly interested
in a stylised running man wearing an animal mask. George noticed the
burned mud structures at the back of the cave, remnants of bins where the
Matabele would have stored their grain during the 1896 uprising or First
Chimurenga. Waves of nausea, increasing in intensity, forced George to
leave the shelter. He stumbled down the slope a few metres and then vom-
ited blood and bile over a rock already spattered with orange lichen. His
action disturbed a group of dassies basking in the early morning sunlight,
and they scattered in all directions.

Once he felt a little better he built a fire in a sheltered spot near the en-
trance to the cave. He made some tea. Polly ate the left-over sadza or
amalaja, which George had put in the ice-cream carton. When she was
full she shared the tea with George. Afterwards he rinsed the carton and
the pot, and stuffed them in the backpack. They still had a long way to go
– about sixty kilometres, as the crow flies, according to Ndiweni – and
George felt sufficiently far enough from Bulawayo to travel by day. The
feeling that his body was finally packing in gave him a new sense of ur-
gency. He put on the backpack and called Polly: "Let's go, kid!"

Ndiweni had advised him to head in the direction of Bambata Cave.
Once they had exited the National Park they would find themselves in
Kumalo Communal Land where people would guide them. The intoxi-
cating beauty of this ancient granite landscape acted as an analgesic on
George, and they reached Bambata, about ten kilometres away, without
his having to rest. He was so thin now that he had to hold his shorts up
as he walked. He eventually devised a makeshift belt with a length of
bark stripped from a mopani sapling. They rested at the picnic site near
Bambata where they could hear running water. They traced the sound to
a nearby spruit and enjoyed themselves paddling, and splashing each

other. George showed Polly how to get clean water by digging in the sand (nature's filter) to below the surface water line. She watched fascinated as the hole gradually filled with clean sweet water. George used the relish pot to scoop it into the Mazoe Orange bottle.

They went on their way. "Look," said George, "an Indaba tree; and it's positively teeming." He guided Polly to a place where she could reach the lower branches, and showed her how to extract the cherry-like fruit from its green capsule. "At Government House in Bulawayo there's a very old specimen – I think it's dead now – of *Pappea capensis*, and it was under the canopy that King Lobengula held meetings with his chiefs. That's why it's called the Indaba tree!" For twenty minutes Polly gorged herself on the refreshing berries. George put one in his mouth, pressed it with his tongue against his palate, and as it burst, the nausea returned. Polly watched with deep concern as he sank to the ground and retched, and retched.

He knew they were out of the National Park when huts, singly or in clusters, began to appear. They saw very few people and even fewer chickens and goats. The immaculately swept surroundings of these villages could not conceal abject poverty, depopulation, inertia. George approached an ancient woman sitting on a grass mat outside her hut, greeted her politely and asked her in halting Ndebele if she knew the way to Empandeni Mission. She pointed in the opposite direction to which they were heading, and George had a mild panic attack. Then he noticed that she was blind, her eyes blue with cataracts. He bade her farewell, took the child's hand and continued, using the sun as his guide, in what he thought was a westerly direction. The sun was not much help at this time of day, squatting more or less directly above the heads of the now weary travellers. Then he heard a welcome sound. Away to the left of their path, the incessant chatter of white-browed sparrow-weavers. When he found their colony, some fifteen nests occupying two adjacent acacia trees, he was amazed to discover that the blind old woman had been right. Somewhere between Bambata and these birds, a distance of about twelve kilometres, George had completely lost his bearings. They had begun heading back to Bambata! Sparrow-weavers nearly always build their nests on the west side of trees, nobody knows for certain why, and George used these large, scruffy constructions to guide him in the right direction.

They made camp, that evening, on the banks of the Shasani River, not far from a seemingly deserted village. The weather was balmy, not a breeze stirred. George made a fire and cooked sadza for Polly. There was no relish but it seemed with relish that Polly consumed the bland porridge. Afterwards George made tea. He could not stomach more than a sip or two. They found a comfortable spot on the river bed and fell asleep under the blanket of the night.

When George woke it was broad daylight. He might have continued sleeping – forever – if the little girl had not decided to weave a garland of flowers in his lank grey hair. She had found yellow aspilia, blue vernonia, and pink stud thorn (Enter, Lear, fantastically dressed with wild flowers). He gave her a long, sighing hug, and she giggled at her handiwork. He asked her to take him to the pink flowers. "Now, my child," he said, "this is *inkunzane*, nature's soap. Look…" He picked a mess of the leaves and stems, taking care to avoid the sharp spines. He rubbed them vigorously in his hands, releasing quantities of slimy sap, which he transferred to Polly's hands and arms, 'soaping' her up to the elbows. She was delighted. "Now you try it." He gave her some fresh leaves mingled with roots and stems. "Rub it hard in your hands and then use it to wash your face and neck." He mimed the action for her.

"Now, let's dig for water so that we can have some breakfast." He noticed, not far from where they had slept, a pool resplendent with blue water lilies. He felt underneath them for tubers and pulled up two. These he scraped clean of fibre and then boiled until they were soft. The tubers were spongy and tasteless but a little pepper and salt would work wonders. Famine food or not, Polly wolfed down the combination of stiff porridge and *Nymphaea caerulea*, flower of the river: *amaleboemfula*, also known as the lotus. "Are you experiencing a pleasant sense of forgetfulness, dear child?" Polly, chewing away, looked at him quizzically. "Have you lost your desire to go home?"

"Let's go home." He killed the fire and packed away the things. Holding hands they crossed the Shashani River and walked, stumbled, walked, stumbled… till they reached a place called Maswaswana where they found marula fruit aplenty, and another colony of sparrow-weavers.

which gave George his bearings. Lying in a foetal position in order to ease the ache in his stomach, away from the marula tree since the smell of the fruit made him nauseous, George felt himself drifting into a sleep, one that not only knits up the ravelled sleeve of care, but expands it into a shroud. He kept himself awake by repeating the last stanza of 'Stopping by Woods on a Snowy Evening', by one of his favourite poets, Robert Frost:

> The woods are lovely, dark and deep,
> But I have promises to keep
> And miles to go before I sleep,
> And miles to go before I sleep...

... you see, girls and boys, two words in the title of the poem point to its theme-

Can't you just give us notes!

... 'stopping' is a present participle, which functions simultaneously as a verb (action) and a noun (inaction)... 'evening' is a time of the day when light and darkness merge... light symbolises life, darkness symbolises death... the poem captures...

Notes! We want notes!

... an epiphanic experience, a moment of eternity, when life and death merge and become what John Keats call the feel of not to feel... it is a paradox...

Why don't you shut your face, you old fart!

... the key phrase in the poem is 'downy flake'... 'down' with its con-notations of warmth... down is a bird's under-plumage used in cushions and sleeping bags...

What's this got to do with our exams?

... and 'flake' with its connotations of cold... here a snowflake... warmth suggests life, and cold suggests death... further...

Notes!

... more, 'down' is downward moving and flake is upward moving... so the phrase captures the merging of opposites... you can see this at work, less beautifully, in the phrase, 'frozen lake'... the paradox here... oxymoron... is a solid liquid... the liquid, water, suggests, life... the solid... ice... or frost suggests death...

Sir, Clifford farted!

… right from the start, the persona intimates that he shouldn't be doing what he is doing… he is trespassing… his horse…

Sis, man, Sir, can't you smell it?

… resists… 'woods' is an archetype of primal fear… go back to the fairy tales of your childhood…

We still children, man, Sir. We need notes!

… and remind yourself how frequently woods feature as the place where people get lost or encounter wolves, ogres, and witches…

Mrs Dube is a witch!

… yet woods are beautiful, numinous, charged with the presence of the unknown… woods unlock your sixth sense, the sense of epiphany, when the unknown is briefly manifested to you…

Sir, Lertitia says Mrs Dube rides you at night!

… the woods represent the persona's death wish… notice he isn't quite in them… he is 'between the woods and frozen lake'… his sub-consciousness… Dionysian… is pulling him towards extinction, while his consciousness… Apollonian… is pulling the other way, telling him that it is not yet time… still miles to go… and promises to keep… sleep is a paradox |for shit's sake, George!| of life and death…

Can't we just have notes?

… the life wish prevails… the pivotal word, 'but' in the final stanza sees to that… it is with reluctance and a certain weariness, however, that the persona continues his journey home… this is evoked by the repetition in the last two lines… in life the merging of opposites is momentary, but in art… in the poem… it is held for…

He realised that Polly was shaking him, gripping his ears, and whimpering. He sat up and took her in his arms. "There, there, sweet girl," he said, "I'll get you home. Not far to go now. We'll go to supper in the morning, and I'll go to bed at noon." The scent of marula fruit on her breath made him gag.

Their next, and final, stop for that day was Mangwe Pass, where the first white settlers entered Matabeleland in 1854. The place was deserted. George remembered reading – was it in Tredgold? – of Robert Moffat's first trek from Kuruman and how there was 'one sad little casualty': a kitten. The first pioneer casualty was a kitten! It must be buried here somewhere, he thought, looking about for a place to camp. Polly scrambled to the summit of the pass to inspect the memorial to the pre-pioneers, but George could not muster the strength to accompany her. He found a sheltered, reasonably level place between two rocky outcrops, and set up camp, which meant making a fire and cooking the last of the mealie meal for Polly. He calculated that they would arrive at Empandeni mission the following evening. He hoped that somebody there would recognise the child or, if not, at least take her in and look after her.

She wanted some more of *The Enormous Turnip* so, before it got too dark for his eyes, George put her on his lap, the book on her lap, and continued:

THE OLD WOMAN PULLS THE OLD MAN AND THE OLD MAN PULLS THE TURNIP. THEY PULL AND PULL, BUT THEY CAN'T PULL UP THE ENORMOUS TURNIP. Hasn't she got a big bottom? And look at her funny shoes! I think they're called clogs. I don't think they are used to hugging each other, do you?

THE OLD WOMAN CALLS TO A BOY. COME AND HELP US TO PULL UP THIS ENORMOUS TURNIP, SHE SAYS. See the little boy on the fence. He is dressed in blue, like your jeans. What do you think he is holding in his right hand? It's a bow and arrow. I wonder what he's been hunting? I hope it isn't the robin redbreast!

THE BOY PULLS THE OLD WOMAN AND... Sorry, sweet child, I can't go on. But if you look at the pictures that follow you will see that the turnip eventually comes up, and all those who helped pull it up, even the humble little mouse, share it, in the spirit of *Harambee*, for dinner.

George lay back exhausted while Polly paged through and through the book, never saying a word but pointing out this and that feature, and sometimes smiling. Now, radiant with health, she was, George noticed with pride, a beautiful child. 'Honour their memory' was inscribed on the memorial to the pre-pioneers, and below it, in fading white paint, 'Florence Partridge woz here.'

For the first time since they had been together, the old man fell asleep before the child.

22

George awoke to a dawn chorus dominated by duetting sparrow-weavers being imitated, at a distance, by fork-tailed drongos. As he tried to sit up, a searing pain spread from his bowels to his head. Polly was still asleep, clinging for warmth and security to George's gaunt body. He lay back and watched a flock of white-backed vultures circling overhead. They had a habit of attacking the eyes and mouth first. They tear holes in the skin to get at the flesh by inserting their heads and necks. George had treasured his well-worn copy of Roberts' *Birds of South Africa*. He thought of all his books and records stacked in crazy piles in the single room of the servant's quarters his grandparents' and parents' succession of servants, mostly 'foreigners' from Malawi and Mozambique, had occupied before George moved in. He smiled at the thought that Beauticious would make very little money from the sale of such worthless objects. Her colleagues read only the *Bulawayo Chronicle* (over and over) and glossy magazines from South Africa. As for music, they all possessed i-pods.

The birds-nests pointed them in a direction, which brought them quite soon to the Mangwe River and there they found breakfast. The many broken shells of sweet monkey orange strewn under the trees and along the river banks indicated that others, human and animal, had feasted before them. But there were still plenty of whole fruits, deep golden-yellow, to be negotiated. George showed Polly how to throw them onto the ground to crack the shells. Then he showed her how to use a piece of the shell as a spoon. In this way she managed to despatch three of the fruits in quick succession. George's nausea returned at the rich, almost sickly smell of the fruits, and he waited for Polly at a distance. Waiting too at a distance, perched on the highest tree in the vicinity, which happened to be dead, was a solitary jackal buzzard.

George gave Polly a little of the water from the Mazoe Orange bottle to wash her face and hands, then they continued on their way through bush that was becoming more and more sparse. The ground was teeming with shiny black Matabele ants stinking of formic acid. George warned Polly to keep away from them since they could bite as well as sting. He needed to rest more and more frequently and this barren terrain provided very little shade. When Polly, who'd been walking in his wake, came up to him and took his hand, he realised he had begun to wander. She dragged him on to a faint pathway with nodding grass on either side. It was the weight of ticks that tipped them over so that when hosts, like George and Polly, brushed past them, the ticks would drop on to their bodies and seek a warm, damp place to feed. Thank goodness Polly had moved to the front, because George in his semi-delirious state would not have noticed the snake lying across the path waiting for a rat or a toad to come along. Polly's sudden intake of breath alerted George to danger. His eyes followed her pointing finger and there, a metre ahead, was the biggest puff adder he had ever seen. The flattened triangular head was pointing in their direction, and its forked tongue was moving rapidly in and out. It was a sandy brown in colour with yellowish V-shaped markings along its back. George put his hands on Polly's shoulders and guided her off the path. "It's all right," he croaked, "it won't bother us if we don't bother it. Cripes, I wish we could find some shade!" He took out the water bottle and let Polly drink her fill. It had about as much water in it as the Chief Inspector had had flat Fanta the night George had given him a lesson on *A Grain of Wheat*. Or was it *Hamlet*?

George came round with his head on Polly's lap. Her tears splashing his face had woken him. His khaki shirt was encrusted with blood and bile, and he seemed to have lost control of his bowels. It took every ounce of his remaining energy to sit up and then stand up. Curiously his fez was still on his head. He had no idea how much further they had walked but he could smell water, and he was desperate to wash himself and his clothes. Polly insisted on carrying the baggage. She walked on purposefully, looking back every now and then to see if he were following her. The distance between them gradually increased. They arrived at a fork of the Ingwizi River and were overjoyed to find that it had clean running water. Polly helped George undress and then helped him into the reviving water. She watched him as he feebly rinsed his clothes and washed his body. She seemed not inclined to join him; instead she located a spot of dry sand nearby and began to dig for water, the way George had showed her. Once enough clean water had seeped into the hole, she unpacked the pot and the water bottle and used the former to fill the latter. As she worked she glanced anxiously at her companion in the river. If he blacked out he would drown.

When he was ready she helped him out of the stream and helped him put on his wet clothes. He was feeling a lot better. He even managed to hold down a sip or two of the water Polly offered him. Then they crossed the river and walked in the direction of the late afternoon sun. They passed through a seemingly deserted village, crossed the second fork of the Ingwizi River, and found themselves on the Empandeni Estate. In the distance they could see the buildings of the mission. When Polly saw a nun, her white habit billowing as she fed some healthy looking chickens, she dropped the backpack and ran, and ran. George watched through tears of joy mingled with relief as the nun put down her tray of seed and opened her arms to the little girl crying, George heard it clearly, "Polly Petal, you have come back! You have come back!"

"Sister!" Polly shouted in reply. It was the first word George had ever heard her speak – and the last. It wasn't a sentence but it was a complete statement.

George turned away and walked, as quickly as he was able, to the river, the first fork where he had rinsed his body and his clothes. There he rested for an hour, until the last light of the sun was replaced by the first light of the moon, not Coleridge's but Byron's:

> So, we'll go no more a roving
> So late into the night,
> Though the heart be still as loving,
> And the moon be still as bright.

He struggled to his feet and continued walking, gasping with pain. He fell so frequently that he no longer sought organised rest. His intention was to keep going until he could go no more. By the time he arrived at Fort Mangwe he was literally crawling on his bloodied hands and knees.

The ruin was surrounded by whispering grass. He managed to climb over the low stone wall into what remained of the enclosure where his grandmother had been born, and there he died.

George had done his duty.